"If the runaway takes this path," B'Elanna said, "it will miss all systems and leave the plane of the galaxy quickly."

Janeway looked at that small area. How in the world were they going to control one of the rarest and most powerful events in nature, enough to send a neutron star along that path?

It didn't seem possible.

But it had to be possible. Otherwise they were about to witness the death of entire systems full of beings. And that wasn't an option.

"Dr. Maalot," she said. "How much time do we have?"

Maalot shrugged. "The separation between the two neutron stars is under seven hundred kilometers now, and the revolutionary period of the two has decreased to under half a second." He seemed to think for a moment, then went on. "Eight hours. I'd count on the eight hours."

"I want ideas in front of me in one hour," Janeway said, her voice as firm as she could make it. "Dismissed."

STAR TREK®
VOYAGER™

DEATH OF A NEUTRON STAR

Eric Kotani
with
Dean Wesley Smith

POCKET BOOKS

New York   London   Toronto   Sydney   Tokyo   Singapore

An *Original* Publication of POCKET BOOKS

POCKET BOOKS, a division of Simon & Schuster Inc. 1230 Avenue of the Americas, New York, NY 10020

This book is published by Pocket Books, a division of Simon & Schuster Inc., under exclusive license from Paramount Pictures.

ISBN: 0-671-00425-5

First Pocket Books printing March 1999

10 9 8 7 6 5 4 3 2 1

POCKET and colophon are registered trademarks of Simon & Schuster Inc.

Printed in the U.S.A.

For
Aileen Boutilier,
David and Lynn Drake,
Dan and Judy Goldin,
George and Carolina McCluskey,
Steve and Renee Wilson,
Jeff Karl,
and
Fouad and Sue Aide

INTRODUCTION

Gene Roddenberry Crater on Mars

At the 42nd triennial General Assembly of the International Astronomical Union (IAU), held in The Hague in 1994, a Martian crater was named in honor of Gene Roddenberry.

The Roddenberry crater is located at Martian latitude −49.9 degrees and longitude 4.5 degrees, in Quad MC26SE on Map I-1682. [Quad defines the name of the map on which it appears and "Map" is the USGS number for that map.] Its diameter is approximately 140 km or about 87 miles. Photograph courtesy of NASA.

DEATH OF A NEUTRON STAR

CHAPTER
1

CAPTAIN KATHRYN JANEWAY SAT IN HER COMMAND chair, staring at the image of the speeding craft on her main screen. Around her the bridge was silent; a waiting silence, a holding-breath silence, as her bridge crew stood or sat at their stations and watched.

At best the small craft was big enough to hold four humans, but the design was nothing Janeway had ever seen before. Swept-back, finlike wings made it seem more like a bird in flight, while its long "nose" curved upward like the front of a water ski. The craft was painted a gold metallic, with black stripes that gave it the sense of motion. It seemed clearly designed for atmospheric use, but it was a long, long way from any atmosphere.

1

Janeway was fascinated by it, especially since it seemed to be in a very great hurry. They had been tracking it from a distance for the last ten minutes, and unless the craft had very good sensors, she doubted that they had even seen *Voyager* yet.

She picked up her half-forgotten cup of coffee and sipped, letting the wonderful flavor fill her mouth. Even barely warm, it was still delicious. Neelix had found some fascinating beans on an uninhabited planet six days earlier, and had managed, for the first time, to really brew a good cup of coffee. It was rich, with an aroma that woke her up and soothed her at the same time. There was only one small problem. Unless they could do a decent replication of the bean, their supply was only going to last another week, especially with most of the crew drinking it. It would be a sad day when the last cup was poured. Until then—hot, warm, or even cold—she wasn't going to waste a drop.

"Can't tell exactly where it's heading, Captain," Harry Kim said, finally breaking the silence.

"It seems to have originated," Tuvok said, "from a planet a few light-years away."

"Sure is a great-looking ship," Tom Paris said. "I'd love to get a look inside."

"I doubt you're going to," Kim said.

Janeway glanced around at her operations officer and took another half sip.

Kim shrugged. "From what I can tell with distant scans, they're overloading the engine."

Janeway set the cup down beside her and stared

at the beautiful and very alien ship on her main viewscreen. "Tom, take us in closer. I want more information."

She turned to Kim. "Ensign, hail them. Let them know we have no hostile intentions."

The bridge again fell silent.

"No response to the hail, Captain," Ensign Kim said.

"Keep at it," she said.

On screen the small ship seemed to grow in size. Janeway studied its lines, swept-back and beautiful. Like Paris, she wanted to see the inside of the thing. But the real question was why was it out here in the first place? And why was it pushing so hard? It was almost as if it were running from something.

She turned to Tuvok. "Do a long-range scan along the path the ship has taken."

Tuvok nodded and set to work.

"Still no response, Captain," Ensign Kim said.

"Captain," Tuvok said. "A large, unidentified ship is on an intercept path. It will overtake the smaller craft in three minutes and seven seconds."

Janeway nodded, then turned back to stare at the beautiful small craft that now filled her screen. So she had her answer as to why the craft was in such a hurry. It was being chased.

"Captain," Ensign Kim said, "the small craft's engines are about to overload."

"How long?"

Kim shook his head. "They'll go critical in thirty seconds, if they aren't shut down."

"Open a hailing frequency," she said, turning back to the screen. "This is Captain Janeway of the Federation starship *Voyager*. You are about to self-destruct. Shut down your engines and we will offer what assistance we can."

"Incoming message from the larger ship," Kim said.

She turned as he glanced up.

"They are demanding that we stand aside."

"They are not our match, Captain," Tuvok said. "In weapons, or in screens."

"Small craft powering down," Kim said.

Janeway nodded. "Mr. Paris, put us directly between the two ships. Ensign Kim, open a three-way conference between us and the two ships."

She turned back to stare at the beautiful small craft, now floating almost dead in space relative to *Voyager*. Her coffee was now completely cold, but she sipped it anyway, waiting, savoring the smooth taste, and wondering what they had gotten into now.

It took a few minutes before she could see the split screen in front of her. The small craft's pilot had features that were essentially human, but with broader forehead and larger green eyes. She looked intense and full of a fighting spirit. Janeway suspected she would like this person, and have trouble with her at the same time. It almost seemed as if sparks had flown from those green eyes.

From what Janeway could see, the small craft's pilot wore what appeared to be a streamlined, dark-red tunic that did little to conceal her athletic upper body. Janeway had watched Tom turn around and raise his eyebrows at Ensign Kim when the alien first appeared. Janeway had ignored the look.

Tuvok had reported that the small craft held only two, and was basically unarmed. Clearly not designed for deep space.

The larger ship, however, was a different story. It had full weapons and screens, and carried a crew of sixty-four beings. Its captain was male, with lizard-like features, slits for eyes, and skin that seemed rough. It was covered with scales. He wore a thin tunic, with weapons banded over his chest. Clearly a warlike race of some sort, at least at first glance.

Janeway spoke up first. "I am Captain Janeway of the Federation starship *Voyager*. We are from another galactic quadrant, here for scientific exploration. We would like to help you resolve your dispute without recourse to violence."

"Captain Qavim of His Imperial Majesty's frigate *Falcon*," the reptilian captain said. "We are pursuing the two rebels who stole a yacht belonging to our royal prince. We demand that you cease your intrusion immediately! Stand aside, or you will suffer the consequences."

"That's completely untrue!" the small craft's pilot said, her eyes even angrier. This woman's anger was not to be taken lightly.

"I am Lieutenant Tyla of the Lekk Deep Space Force. Lekks are *not* a subject race in the Qavok

Empire." She faced Janeway directly. "They kidnapped us; we were trying to escape from their captivity."

"Nonsense!" Qavim said, a snort of disgust clear as thin flaps where his nose was flared open. "Your political leaders are voluntary guests in our world, preparing to take an oath of allegiance to the Emperor."

Lieutenant Tyla looked at the Qavok captain in utter disbelief. "Lies! All lies! You Qavoks abducted our First Citizen and his cabinet members under deception, and took them to one of your miserable planets. Forced incarceration and coercion are a lot different from voluntarily taking a pledge of fealty!"

Turning her attention back to Janeway, Tyla went on, "When the abduction took place, Dr. Maalot and I happened to be at the Congress Hall and were captured by sheer bad luck."

Janeway glanced over Tyla's shoulder to where the other passenger of the small craft stood, looking timid. Clearly he was the Dr. Maalot she had mentioned.

"We commandeered this yacht and made a getaway. We are now trying to get home fast and warn our people about the Qavok plan. If we give them enough time, they might be able to stop it. At least save some lives."

"So you attempted a suicidal interstellar journey home with a small vessel designed basically for interplanetary trips?" Janeway asked.

Tyla stood firm, her jaw jutting out more than before. "We did what we felt we must to save our people."

Janeway nodded. She could see the clear determination in Tyla's eyes. For the moment Janeway was willing to accept Tyla's version of the events. The Qavok captain, on the other hand, was pushing the envelope. Janeway compressed her lips in irritation.

"The Lekk woman is telling you a child's tale, Captain. It is a waste of time to listen to her. If you do not remove your ship within the next five minutes, we will destroy your ship and take the yacht. It will be the same to us either way."

"Captain Qavim," Janeway said, turning to face him squarely. "If attacked, we will defend ourselves. Do I make myself clear?"

"We have the right to our property," he said, seemingly sneering at her, if she was interpreting his expression correctly.

"Any attempt to destroy or capture the other craft before a peaceful resolution is reached will be regarded as a hostile military action against us." Janeway stared at him, not blinking. "Trust that we will respond accordingly."

The Qavok captain's eye slits seemed to enlarge slightly; then he cut off, leaving only Tyla on the screen.

"Stand ready," Tyla said to Janeway. "He will not wait the five minutes. He will attack."

"Thank you," Janeway said, smiling. "We can take care of ourselves. You just hold your position."

"Thank you, Captain," Tyla said, and cut the connection.

Janeway turned to Chakotay and nodded.

"Shields up," he said. "Stand by weapons."

Janeway sat down in her chair as the first volley of the Qavok's directed-energy weapons hit *Voyager*.

"Short five minutes," Tom said.

"The guy's predictable," Janeway said, holding her coffee cup to keep what was left of it from spilling in the slight shaking.

"Screens holding," Chakotay said. "One hundred percent."

"No report of damage, Captain," Kim said.

"Return fire," she ordered. "Target their weapons only. We don't want to destroy them and start an all-out war."

It took only five quick shots, less than three seconds, before the Qavok frigate was disarmed.

"Cease fire," Janeway said. "Hail Captain Qavim."

"Hailing, Captain," Kim said.

A few moments passed. "No response, Captain."

Janeway leaned back in her chair and sipped her cold but still wonderful coffee. "We'll just let him sit for a minute," she said. "Give him time to have a cup of coffee and think over his options."

* * *

On the bridge of the Qavok frigate, reports of damage poured in. A faint smell of smoke filled the air, and Qavim's junior officers standing at three stations seemed far too excited for their own good. Excited officers are reckless officers, he thought. He would have them replaced later.

"Gun Turret Number One totally destroyed!" Qubo, his executive officer, said. "No survivors."

"Go on," Qavim said.

"Gun Turret Number Two completely demolished. No crew reporting in. All presumed dead."

Qavim nodded and the list of damage continued. The naturally cheerless atmosphere of the Qavok bridge was now grim. Only the executive officer's voice droned on through the faint smoke and smell of burnt wires.

Qavim partially listened while thinking back over the last few minutes. He had underestimated his enemy. He would not make that mistake again, providing there was an "again." Surviving to have another chance at that ship would have to be his priority.

After the list of damage was finished, he stood up from his captain's chair as if trying to regain a measure of control over his destiny.

"They hail us, Captain."

"No response," he said, staring at the screen and the alien ship floating between him and the yacht. "Withdraw from the combat zone immediately."

"Yes, Captain!" His executive officer executed the order without delay.

As the ship turned and moved off, Qavim again sat down in his command chair. He had made a mistake that should have gotten them killed. For all he knew, *Voyager*'s captain could have been as bloodthirsty as many of his fellow officers in the Qavok Space Forces. She might still come after his frigate to finish it off, if he provoked her sufficiently. But he didn't feel she would. He had been taught that retreat could be the wisest course of action under some circumstances. Not often, but now seemed to be one of those times.

He would retreat, repair their weapons, and possibly watch from a safe distance for the next move *Voyager* would make. The fact that his enemy only disarmed his frigate signaled to him that the Federation ship did not wish to engage his powerful vessel in battle. This *Voyager* captain was wise.

But now was not the time to let professional respect get in the way of his plan to exact revenge from *Voyager*. The real question was, how he could pass the buck for his own failure to recapture the prince's yacht. The *Voyager* captain was no longer his immediate enemy. It was certain that someone's head would roll. His task now was to make sure that rolling head was someone else's.

"Orders?" Qubo asked.

"Start repairs on weapons. Hold position."

He watched his men start to work, then went back to the most important problem facing him: survival. Would the admiral believe it if he said his ship had been ambushed? No, that would probably not work. Nobody would believe that the renegade Lekks would have been able to set up an ambush in advance of their escape. Especially not in interstellar space. He needed a story that would be corroborated by his crew, or at least not refuted by the ship's records.

There was no doubt that Qubo was looking for an opportunity to take over as captain. There was no way that Qubo would lie for Qavim; by simply telling the truth he would be in line for promotion. That thought gave Qavim an idea. Suppose he made his executive a collaborator with the Lekks? His mind started working on a scenario that might convince the admiral. Qavim would first tell Qubo a story that was calculated to cause him to compromise himself. And, then, he would see where that would lead. With luck, he would return with ten ships and destroy this *Voyager*.

"Return to home base," he ordered. "Pace one."

"Captain," Ensign Kim said. "The Qavok ship has jumped to warp, heading back in the direction it came."

"Giving up, or going for reinforcements?" Janeway said. "I'd wager on the latter."

"So would I," Paris said.

"The yacht apparently suffered damage during the pursuit," Chakotay said. "It's going to need some major work on the engines."

Janeway nodded. "Is the yacht small enough to

be brought into our shuttlebay with the tractor beam?"

Chakotay glanced at his screen, then nodded.

"Fine. Do it and let me know when it's aboard. I want to talk to our guests."

Chakotay only nodded as he set to work.

Janeway stood and took her empty coffee cup. "I'll be having a word with Mr. Neelix."

Chakotay glanced up at her and smiled. "Don't worry, B'Elanna will find a way to replicate the coffee."

"I sure hope so," she said, laughing. "But until then, I'm not missing my second cup for anything."

Tyla watched the Qavok ship retreat in disbelief. In all her years, she would have never imagined such a day. But she would have also never imagined being captured and then escaping in the Qavok prince's royal yacht, either.

She dropped down into one of the plush chairs and looked around. She felt comically incongruent in the posh quarters of the princely yacht. The tapestries on the walls of the living quarters alone must have cost more than she had earned in her entire life. Even the simple boxes on the dressing cabinets were inlaid with gold and encrusted with glittering jewelry.

Unfortunately, the lavish extras hid no console for weapons systems in the ship. Judging from the absence of anything warlike, Tyla assumed the ship was never intended to travel any great distances without a military escort of some sort. The yacht was clearly designed solely for the comfort and privacy of the prince and his guests.

Tyla had laughed as she searched the vessel. The prince's taste in women was truly ecumenical, judging from the various holophotos of Qavok women in various stages of undress. She wondered how many of them were his wives. Or were they just slaves, like the Lekks were supposed to become.

The small ship jerked slightly as the alien ship *Voyager* took it under control.

Tyla glanced at Dr. Maalot and tried to nod reassuringly. This Captain Janeway looked trustworthy, but too much was riding on how Tyla handled matters next. If she could reach an understanding with the captain of the *Voyager*, she might be able to get home in time to save her homeworld.

Tom Paris watched as the bay doors closed behind the flowing lines of the Qavok yacht. He'd seen a lot of beautiful ships, but this one was right up there near the top of the list. He wanted to just go over and stroke the gold- and silver-plated surface. Even sitting on the deck, the ship looked as if it wanted to fly, as if it were speeding through a blue sky over a calm ocean.

But he didn't move. Instead he stood waiting

alone as the door in the side of the yacht slid silently open and Lieutenant Tyla stepped out onto the deck, followed by a Lekk man.

Tom felt the tightness in his chest as Tyla stopped and looked around the bay, then turned and strode toward him. She was gorgeous, in a dark red tunic and black tights. The tunic accented her bright red hair. Even more beautiful than she had appeared on the screen.

Behind him the door to the shuttlebay slid open and Seven of Nine entered, moving to his side.

He forced himself to swallow and then smile, making sure Tyla had a friendly face to greet her.

"Welcome to *Voyager*," he said, stepping forward and extending his hand.

The vivacious redhead grasped his arm firmly when he extended his hand toward her. Apparently, an arm-grasp, quite similar to that practiced in ancient Rome, was the Lekk custom of greeting, at least in their military.

"I'm Lieutenant Paris. Tom," he said. "Welcome aboard *Voyager*."

"Second Lieutenant Tyla of the Lekk Deep Space Force," she said. Her gaze held his for a moment, and then she smiled. "A real pleasure!"

Turning toward her passenger, she added, "This is Dr. Maalot, ship's astrophysicist."

"Seven of Nine," Tom said, taking a deep breath and forcing himself to do his share of introductions.

"A Borg?" Maalot asked, somewhat shocked.

"I was with the Collective, once," Seven said. "I am no longer."

Tom managed not to smile. He'd seen Seven go through this sort of introduction a number of times now.

Maalot nodded; then with one long, last gaze at Seven, he turned back toward Tom.

"Lieutenant Paris," Tyla said, moving to a more formal posture. "I must report to your captain. I have important information your ship will need if the Qavoks return in force."

"I don't see a problem with that," Tom said, smiling at Tyla. "But first the captain ordered me to see to it that you two receive medical attention, if needed."

"Thank you, Lieutenant," Tyla said, relaxing a little and touching his arm again. "But we are fine. We are most anxious to talk to your captain immediately."

Tom wished he had an excuse to delay her for just a little while longer. But duty called.

"And your science officer," Dr. Maalot said. "Since much of my report is of an astrophysical nature, I will need to talk to a science officer."

"I think the captain will, most likely, be the best person on both counts."

"I will also be able to supply needed information," Seven said.

"Good," Dr. Maalot said, again glancing somewhat fearfully at the Borg. "There isn't much time left."

Paris glanced at Tyla, who only shrugged. "He's right."

"I think *Voyager* can handle the Qavok ships," Tom said.

"It's not the ships I'm worried about," Dr. Maalot said. "It's the dying neutron stars."

Seven stepped forward suddenly and faced Dr. Maalot, towering over him. "Explain."

Tom pulled Seven back gently by the arm. "I think it would be better to tell it all to the captain."

Seven glanced at Tom, then nodded and turned toward the bay entrance without saying a word.

Tyla and Dr. Maalot both looked a little shocked.

Tom smiled and shrugged. "She gets a little excited when science comes up."

"So should we all, Mr. Paris," said Maalot, whose tone reminded Tom of one of his stuffier professors at the Academy.

"Uh, yes, well. Please come this way," he replied, gesturing for the two to follow him. They did, at a distance. This was going to be a long day.

CHAPTER
2

Janeway had just finished the last of her second cup of coffee when Paris escorted their two guests onto the bridge.

Tyla looked around, taking in all that she saw. She was a striking officer, with her red hair and tunic, but Janeway's gaze was drawn more immediately to the man with her. He was Dr. Maalot, she presumed. Like Tyla, he had deep green eyes. But unlike Tyla, with her confident demeanor, his eyes were filled with worry. Deep worry. How did two such different personalities end up escaping together?

Janeway rose from her command chair and moved up toward her guests. Tyla stepped forward, directly in front of Janeway, with Maalot hanging back a little.

"Captain, I don't know how we can thank you," she started off saying. "If you would just help us get our ship repaired, we'll be gone as quickly as possible."

Janeway waved the lieutenant's comments aside. "You needed help and we were close by. I assume this is the Dr. Maalot you spoke of?"

Tyla nodded and turned as Maalot took half a step forward and stood in front of the captain. "A pleasure meeting you, Captain. And thank you from all our people."

"Glad to have you both aboard. Please follow me. We'll go where we can talk."

Janeway led her two guests into the meeting room off the bridge. For some reason Dr. Maalot was bothering her. There was something disturbing about the Lekk doctor that she couldn't put a finger on.

Chakotay, Paris, Ensign Kim, Seven, and B'Elanna joined them. Janeway waited until all were seated, then turned to Lieutenant Tyla.

"I'd like a brief account of how you have ended up in this situation? If you wouldn't mind?"

"Captain," Dr. Maalot broke in. "I fear the neutron-star situation is approaching a critical point, if only I—"

Janeway cut him off with a raised hand. "First things first, Doctor, if you don't mind. I have a military situation on my hands here and that must be dealt with first. It will only take a moment, I'm sure."

Maalot swallowed and nodded.

Tyla glanced at her companion, then faced Janeway. Janeway could see sparks of irritation in the woman's eyes. She wasn't exactly happy at the moment. Probably because Janeway had ignored her request to have the yacht fixed.

After a moment's hesitation, Tyla started into her report. "The Qavoks have been scheming to annex our planetary system into their empire for decades, but their first outward actions began about a year ago when they attacked the heart of our home system."

"You beat them back," Janeway said.

Tyla smiled, the memory of the victory obviously a good one. "Soundly," she said "They were humiliated."

Janeway nodded. "So what happened next?"

Tyla's smile faded. "We are not naturally a military people, Captain. After we won, our leaders saw little option but to negotiate. Many of us disagreed, but we lacked the means to counterattack."

Janeway nodded sympathetically. Maintaining the balance between peace and force was the hardest part of her job and any other Starfleet captain's. It had taken humans centuries to learn that balance.

"During an initial meeting two weeks ago," Tyla

said, "they deceived our political leaders and abducted them. Our leaders were all taken to one of the Qavok planets, and are now hostages there. Dr. Maalot and I happened to be present in the Congress Hall for an astrophysical report when the kidnapping occurred, and we too were captured."

Janeway saw where Tyla's report was leading. "I see. You and Dr. Maalot, then, are the only people who managed to escape?"

The lieutenant nodded. "Yes, Captain, so far as we know. There is something I must make clear here. My people are in a state of war with the Qavoks. I believe the yacht is rightly a spoil of the war. I have no intention of returning it."

Janeway raised her eyebrows, surprised at the seemingly sudden demands. The woman clearly had courage, but not much working knowledge of diplomacy.

"That issue will be settled later," Janeway said. "I'm sure we can come to some agreement. How long were you in flight?"

Tyla started to say something, then snapped her mouth shut. Her face turned almost as red as her hair. Janeway knew right at that moment the woman was going to be trouble.

Janeway maintained eye contact until Tyla finally answered. "One full day, at top speed."

"So at least two full days for Qavim to get back to his base, regroup, and come back to this location with more ships."

Tyla nodded. "At least. If he doesn't get executed

for failing when he reports back. It is a Qavok tradition. Kill all failures."

"Couldn't happen to a nicer guy," Paris said.

Chakotay frowned at him and Janeway ignored the comment.

"Anything else you can think of that might help us in a fight with the Qavoks?"

Tyla shook her head.

Janeway nodded and turned. "Okay, Doctor, it seems we have a little time. It's your turn. How about starting at the beginning so we follow you?"

Dr. Maalot nodded, swallowed hard, then said, "This might be a little technical."

"We'll manage," Janeway said, glancing at where Seven sat, staring at the doctor.

He glanced at Seven also, then started. "Two weeks ago I was on a medium-sized asteroid near the outer edge of our home system, tinkering with a signal-enhancing device attached to a large array of radio antennae. I detected weak, rapidly variable, periodic signals from a binary pulsar."

"Binary pulsar?" Janeway asked, leaning forward. "Those are very, very rare."

Dr. Maalot could only nod. "From its extremely short orbital period of barely eight seconds, I immediately deduced the nature of this neutron-star pair. Judging from the binary system's high relative velocity with respect to the local stars, the pair might have been ejected from a triple-star system through a cataclysmic event of some sort."

Maalot sounded quite proud of his discovery, as

he had every right to be, as far as Janeway was concerned. What he had found was one of the rarest things in known space.

"A pulsar binary with such a short orbital period?" Seven asked. "Are you certain?"

"Yes," Maalot said. "Its orbit must be decaying rapidly through gravitational radiation."

"Allowing for the light transit time to your homeworld," Janeway said, "the period would already have to be much shorter at the source now."

"Correct," Maalot said, clearly delighted with the knowledgeable questions. Janeway understood such delight. For one thing, most people did not understand that what one observed with a telescope was what had happened at the source some time ago; if the star was located a dozen light-years away, what you were observing had already happened there a dozen years before.

"The distance to the binary pulsar," Maalot said, "from my original observations, turned out to be a little over ten light-years."

"Ten light-years?" Janeway said.

Maalot smiled. "The discovery was thanks mainly to my new signal-enhancing device, at that."

Janeway nodded. "Go on."

"The orbital period was already down to about a second at the source. That shocked me, I must say, Captain. As you can understand, we are facing a possible imminent disaster."

Janeway glanced at Seven, who seemed puzzled at the doctor's fear of disaster.

"The rate of decrease naturally depends on individual masses," Seven said. "You must have determined the masses of the component stars."

Maalot allowed himself to look a little smug before answering the question. "Yes, indeed, I did. What with such a short period, I had the radial velocity curves for each star almost as soon as the discovery was made. The binary system's orbital inclination was also easy to determine; as the two stars eclipsed each other, the orbit was edge-on toward our solar system. It was simple then to calculate the absolute masses; it was one solar mass for the massive star and a tenth of the solar mass for the secondary. The rate of its orbital decay is accelerating at a tremendous rate now."

Janeway nodded.

Beside her Paris looked completely confused, and Chakotay was looking puzzled.

"I need more data," Seven said, "but this seems to indicate that the final stage for the neutron stars could come within a matter of days."

Janeway watched as Maalot stared in clear amazement at Seven. Janeway knew how he felt. Seven could do calculations faster than anyone else aboard.

"That's right," Maalot said. "I had only some preliminary data before taking this report to our political leaders, but the timing should be in that approximate range. Maybe even sooner. And, of course, this orbital inclination gives us a great deal of concern for our solar system."

"Why?" Chakotay said.

Dr. Maalot only looked at him with a frown.

"If this follows pattern," Janeway said, "then the less massive secondary neutron star, which is actually larger in diameter than the primary, will start shedding its exterior mass. Or it might have already started. Correct?"

"Correct, Captain," Maalot said.

"So I too do not understand your worry, exactly."

Seven started to speak, but Janeway stopped her. "I want to hear the doctor's theory."

Maalot nodded. "The lesser star will become a mini-supernova."

"Exactly," Seven said.

"I know that," Janeway said. "Go on."

"When that happens to the companion, the more massive star will turn into a runaway object that will fly away at a relativistic speed in the direction it happens to be headed at the time of the explosion."

"Correct," Seven again said.

Maalot went on as if she had not spoken. "The fugitive star will destroy any solar system in its path, although I have not yet been able to figure out which direction it will take."

"It would not be possible to predict exactly, as yet," Seven said.

"And your homeworld is along one possible path," Chakotay said.

"That is correct," Dr. Maalot said.

"Is there more?" Janeway asked. She could tell that Dr. Maalot wasn't telling them everything.

Maalot glanced at the silent Tyla, then went on. "I just fear that the runaway star will hit our system. I fear for my family and our people. All of them."

Janeway wasn't going to get what he was hiding just yet, that much was clear. She glanced around the room. "Well, we're here to see new things. I for one, have never seen a binary neutron star system in its last days. In fact, I know of no Federation ship that has seen one. Who knows what we might learn."

There were nods throughout the room.

"Mr. Paris, get the coordinates of the binary system from the doctor and set a course. There's no point in us being here when the Qavok return for vengeance."

"Aye, Captain," he said, smiling. He stood, indicating that Dr. Maalot should follow him back to the bridge.

Janeway waited until the two had left the room, then turned to face Tyla directly. "This means we will have no time to take you two back to your homeworld first. However, I promise to do so as soon as we are able to."

"Would it be possible for you to repair my ship and send me on my way?"

Janeway shook her head. "Based on the preliminary assessment of the damage to the yacht, it will take some time to get it back to warp capabilities. We'll do our best, but I'm afraid you're along for the ride at the moment."

Janeway also wanted her chief engineer to have the time to take that yacht apart, so that they would have a reliable appraisal of the Qavok technology in case there should be another armed confrontation with them. It never hurt to be prepared.

Tyla looked almost angry, her green eyes showing her defiance and strong will. "Can we at least attempt to contact my people?"

"Of course," Janeway said. "But I can't imagine them not knowing your leaders have been taken."

Tyla again looked uncomfortable. Janeway waited for a moment, then resigned herself to the fact that she wasn't about to get any more out of Tyla than she had gotten from Maalot. At least not yet.

"Thank you, Captain."

"In the meantime," Janeway said, "I'd appreciate any suggestions about dealing with the Qavok if we run into them along the way."

Tyla nodded. "Understood, Captain. I will do what I can to help your cause."

"And I yours," Janeway said.

Tyla only nodded.

Janeway knew that Tyla didn't like her decision. She frowned as she imagined the hotheaded young woman stealing one of *Voyager*'s shuttlecraft, just as she had stolen the yacht.

"Come with me," Janeway said, standing and heading toward the bridge. As she entered, Tom said, "Course laid in, Captain."

"Let's go," she said. "Warp seven." Then she turned to Dr. Maalot. "Would you be willing to provide my people with information about this star while we are in transit?"

Maalot's face beamed with excitement. "With great pleasure, Captain. I would not have it any other way."

She nodded to Seven and B'Elanna. "Get to it."

Then she turned to Tuvok. "Please escort Tyla to guest quarters."

"Captain, I—"

Janeway held up her hand and stopped the Lekk from speaking. "We have time. Now you need some rest."

Tyla's face again turned a faint shade of red; then she nodded and followed Tuvok off the bridge.

"I don't think she's too happy with that order, Captain," Chakotay said, smiling, as Janeway slumped down into her command chair and stared wistfully at the empty coffee cup.

"Put a security detail near her quarters, but not close enough to be obvious."

Chakotay turned to follow her order.

"And one more thing," she said, staring at the warp images flashing past on the front screen.

"Yes, Captain," Chakotay said.

"I think we both need a cup of coffee." She smiled.

Chakotay laughed softly. "I'll see what Neelix has left."

"Thanks," Janeway said. She sighed, rested her chin on her hand, and looked out at the starscape that lay ahead.

CHAPTER
3

SINCE THERE WAS OVER A DAY UNTIL THEIR ARRIVAL AT the binary star system, Neelix suggested he serve a late lunch first for the officers and the ship's guests. Janeway had figured it wouldn't hurt, and would even give her a little time to get a better sense of the truth of their story. And maybe find out that last detail Dr. Maalot seemed to be hiding.

Now Neelix buzzed around the two Lekks like a mother hen over her chicks. "Don't be shy, friends," Neelix said, putting more food on Dr. Maalot's plate. "There's more, a lot more, where this comes from."

Neelix had seated them all at the same table, with Tyla and Maalot to Janeway's right, Chakotay, Tuvok, B'Elanna, and Paris around the rest of the table. They were the only ones in the mess hall and the meal seemed to go well, as far as Janeway was concerned. But the conversation was purely social. It was time to get down to business.

"Doctor Maalot," she said, "would you mind fielding a few more questions from my officers about the neutron stars?"

Maalot, who had been fiddling around with the last of his pastry with a fork, smiled, then glanced around at the others. "Most assuredly, Captain."

The Lekk astrophysicist seemed almost beside himself to have the opportunity to elucidate on his favorite subject. "Let me begin with the construction of the star."

"The nuclear degenerate matter in a typical neutron star is so densely packed," he said, holding his palms together to illustrate, "that electrons are pushed into protons, turning them into neutrons. Since the star is basically made up of neutrons, instead of all sorts of atoms, as is the case with normal stars, it is called a neutron star. Under these conditions, the density of the matter is a few billion tons per cubic centimeter, which is about the size of a sugar cube. This may sound counterintuitive, but a neutron star with smaller mass is in fact larger in size than a more massive one."

Janeway was surprised the doctor had said all that without even taking a breath. She glanced at Tom. Clearly, the good doctor had almost lost him in the first sentence. Starfleet had required all its officers to take basic astrophysics classes, but they weren't pushed much for pilots.

"I understand that a neutron star's mass is not so different from that of an ordinary star," Ensign Kim said. "But practically every book and article I've read about neutron stars mentions the destructiveness of the tidal force in its vicinity. Why?"

Janeway almost wanted to laugh as Maalot beamed the smile of a happy professor fielding questions from a bright student. "An excellent question! The strength of a gravitational field is in proportion to the total mass of the gravitating body, but it is also inversely—note 'inversely'—proportional to the square of the distance from it."

Paris's eyes widened in confusion and anxiety.

B'Elanna smiled and patted his hand, but Tom ignored her.

Dr. Maalot kept smiling, but nodded. "I'm sorry. Let me put it this way. A neutron star is typically only about ten kilometers in radius—in contrast to the radius of a main-sequence G-type star, whose radius is measured upward of a million kilometers. Thus, an object can get quite close to that great mass of a neutron star. Closer than a ship could ever go to a normal star."

"Which then makes the gravitational force a ship experiences even more tremendous," Janeway said.

"Exactly," Maalot said. "What's more, the tidal force increases in inverse proportion to the cube of the distance from the center of the mass. Thus, any ordinary matter approaching a neutron star too closely would be ripped apart by the inexorable tidal force in its proximity."

"Almost before it knew what hit it," B'Elanna said.

Tom looked even more puzzled. "Put it this way," Janeway said. "Even if a ship were made of a mythical, indestructible *unobtanium*, it and everything and everyone inside the ship would be torn apart at a molecular level if the ship went too close."

Even Kim was starting to look perplexed now. "Ensign, you're not following this?" Janeway asked.

"No, I understand," Kim said, "but how can you have a binary neutron star system? It seems to me that one companion, or the other—possibly both—would be torn apart by the tidal force of the companion."

"Another good question," Dr. Maalot said, again smiling. "Theory is that neutron stars are so tightly bound by their own formidable gravitational field that they can orbit around each other forming a binary pair without being torn up by the other."

"Their intense gravity serves to hold them together," Janeway said.

"Exactly," Dr. Maalot said.

Kim nodded.

"But only up to a certain point of proximity," Dr. Maalot said. "When the two stars are nearly in contact with each other, all hell can, and does, break loose."

"Like any two colliding stars," Paris said.

"No," Dr. Maalot said. "Much worse."

"Not even on the same scale," B'Elanna said.

Janeway nodded. "You have to understand how a neutron star is formed. They are the final stage in the evolution of massive stars, usually formed in the collapsing core of a supergiant after the star has exhausted its fuel. The colossal amount of energy released in such a core collapse propels the enveloping atmosphere explosively away."

"So, basically, this is a supernova," Chakotay said.

Janeway nodded.

"And that leaves a neutron star in its place?" Tom asked.

"Exactly," Janeway said.

"Got it," Paris said.

Janeway glanced around. Kim nodded. Dr. Maalot gestured for her to continue. "A neutron star might also be formed, if a white dwarf star becomes too massive by accreting matter from a companion, and exceeds the upper mass limit for a white dwarf. It would then collapse under its own weight and become a neutron star."

"Was that how this binary was formed?" Paris asked.

The doctor shrugged. "We can't say for sure how this particular pair came into being. In fact, we have little idea how such a pair would ever form."

Janeway nodded. "One of the rarest things in all the universe."

"So," Kim said, "why is, as you put it, all hell going to break loose?"

Dr. Maalot actually laughed. Janeway watched as Lieutenant Tyla just frowned. She had heard all of this before and was apparently trying to tune it out.

Neelix refilled Janeway's cup of coffee again, and she smiled at him.

"A neutron star can lose matter from its surface under the powerful gravitational influence of another neutron star," Dr. Maalot said.

Kim nodded. "I understand that."

"Good. When the two neutron stars get very close to each other, one star's mass could become small enough that it is no longer massive enough to keep its neutron matter in that highly condensed nuclear degenerate form. Destabilized gravitationally, the whole star will explode with a force that is comparable to a small supernova."

"Just how energetic an explosion is a supernova?" Kim asked.

"Best way to explain it is this," Janeway said. "In a typical supernova explosion, energy equivalent to the ordinary radiation from billions of stars is released. That energy is so incomprehensibly immense, even a small percentage of it—as would happen in the explosion of such an underweight neutron star—is still a cosmic cataclysm."

"Does that mean the planetary system of Dr. Maalot and Lieutenant Tyla is doomed?" Paris asked.

Janeway glanced at Dr. Maalot while shaking her head. He also was shaking his head.

"Not necessarily," he said. "Not even probably, at least from the initial explosion. Any planetary system located within a light-year or so of the mini-supernova would be in serious trouble. First, at such a proximity the planet would be exposed to an intense high-energy radiation that would harm animal and plant life. Any technological society would suffer from the electromagnetic pulsation effects precipitated in the atmosphere by the gamma-ray bursts; the EMP effects would shut down all unprotected electronics."

Janeway agreed, but she knew that wasn't all that would happen. "A planet within a light-year would also be hit by a wave of highly energetic plasma. It would be devastating."

"Fortunately," Dr. Maalot said, "our system is just over ten light-years away, where the supernova blast will be considerably diluted. The Lekk world will likely survive the calamity, although there may be some unavoidable damage to our ecological system."

"So, the main danger to your system, Doctor," Janeway said, "involves the direction that the runaway neutron star will take. Am I correct?"

"You are entirely right, Captain. The chances that the runaway star will destroy any particular solar system within ten light-years—by a random chance of the timing of the explosion—are not very high."

"But actually," B'Elanna said, "the runaway star doesn't need to go through the center of a system to destroy it."

"Correct," Dr. Maalot said. "Simply by passing too close, the massive object would alter the planetary orbits so much that the solar system would become uninhabitable. Even with that, the chances for serious calamity on the Lekk planetary system are less than one in a thousand."

"Little comfort to your people, I'll bet," Paris said.

"You've got that right," Tyla said, speaking for the first time in a while. She stretched her long arms. "Doctor, don't you think it's about time you tell these people the real problem? Tell them why I need to get home and warn our people."

Janeway glanced at Tyla, then at Dr. Maalot. It was a good thing the young lieutenant had a lower tolerance for keeping secrets than her companion. It was indeed, about time that *Voyager*'s guests laid their cards on the table.

The doctor looked almost uncomfortable. His green eyes stared down at his coffee cup. After a long moment he spoke without looking up. "We overheard a plan to force the neutron star explosion and send the rogue neutron star into our system."

"What?" Janeway said.

"That's not possible," B'Elanna said.

"I agree," Dr. Maalot said. "I don't think it is possible."

"But that is the Qavoks' plan," Tyla said.

The stunned silence filled the room. There was nothing more to say. There was nothing more Janeway could think of to say. What he had suggested was plainly impossible.

Yet the Qavoks seemed to think they might be able to do it.

Impossible.

Yet . . .

CHAPTER
4

WHEN THE LUNCHEON WAS OVER, JANEWAY, WITH B'Elanna, escorted Dr. Maalot down to the laboratory to start fashioning scientific instruments for the coming expedition near the binary neutron star. This event was going to require some special instruments, and Janeway didn't want to miss any of it, Qavok ships or not.

She was still having problems with the notion that the Qavoks seemed to think they could actually control a neutron star explosion. The scale of such control seemed beyond anything possible for the Federation, let alone a race like the Qavok. And then to use such a thing to destroy an entire homeworld system of an enemy. It was barbaric almost beyond comprehension.

In the lab Seven of Nine was already working, bent over a panel, focused. She didn't even bother to look up as they came in. Janeway smiled. Typical of Seven.

As a first step in Dr. Maalot's quick orientation, Janeway showed him various astrophysical instruments that were already being used on *Voyager*. The first device she showed him was an X-ray imaging-spectrometer; the business end of the equipment—the X-ray detector itself—was mounted outside the ship. Within a few minutes, Maalot not only understood how the device worked, but was offering suggestions on how to enhance its time-resolution capability and dynamical range to make it more suitable for observing the rapidly varying emission from the neutron-star pair.

After an hour of intensive work together in the laboratory, Janeway, Maalot, Seven, and Torres had laid out a viable observing strategy for the binary neutron star.

"Let me review what we have got now," Janeway said, brushing hair back off her forehead. "We will, by the time we arrive, have the correct instruments modified to make observations in all electromagnetic wavelengths."

Torres nodded.

"All the way from gamma-ray to radio frequencies. In all instances we need to improve the time-resolution of existing detectors."

"Correct," Seven said.

"The gravitational wave detector will be a challenge," B'Elanna said, frowning.

"I am confident that we are up to the task," Seven said.

"Given the short time?" Janeway asked. She had her doubts if it could all be done, but something was better than nothing at this point.

Seven glanced at her. "The shortness of the time will pose difficulties, but I can have the task finished."

"Good," Janeway said, smiling and nodding. She knew that if Seven said something would be done, it would be done.

"I'll set up the observation program," Torres said. "We should be ready to start making preliminary observations in a few hours, at most. By the time we arrive at the binary, at any rate, every detector should be tested and operating."

Dr. Maalot bowed slightly toward B'Elanna, looking very formal as he spoke. "Lieutenant Torres, I would be delighted to assist you in this task. I am handy in jobs of this sort, if I may say so myself."

Janeway managed to not laugh at his sudden formality.

With a glance at Janeway, B'Elanna said, "Thank you, Dr. Maalot, I'll be happy to take you up on your offer."

"Let Chakotay know if you need more help," Janeway said. "He will see to it."

"Good," B'Elanna said.

"And when you are set up and ready, please report to my ready room," Janeway said. "I've got something I want to talk to you about."

B'Elanna glanced at her, then nodded.

"Seven, you come, too."

Seven didn't bother to look up from the panel she was working on. B'Elanna again only nodded, but she clearly looked puzzled.

"I'll explain when you get there," Janeway said. Then she turned and headed for the bridge, her thoughts already racing ahead to the binary neutron star, and what it might mean for them.

"This binary could be the break we have been looking for," Janeway said, as much to herself as to Torres and Seven as she paced behind her desk. "We might, just might, find a way to reach Federation space faster with the use of this binary system."

"How so, Captain?" B'Elanna asked.

"Over the past two hours I've gone back over some papers in the field of relativistic astrophysics, including several seminal papers on theoretical gravitational radiation from neutron-star binaries."

Both Seven and B'Elanna said nothing, so she went on. "In one of the last two papers in the series, a theoretically possible device is described for storing up the tremendous energy emitted by a close neutron-star pair in the form of gravitational waves, manifesting themselves as traumatic disturbances in the space-time continuum. The author of the paper thought it possible, but extremely unlikely, that there would be an opportunity to actually test the device in real life."

"But we now have that opportunity, don't we, Captain?" B'Elanna said, shaking her head. "I don't think we need any more on our plate, to be honest. It's going to be——"

Janeway held up her hand for Torres to stop. "You don't understand what I'm getting at."

"Captain," Seven said. "I am at a loss, also. The orbital energy and the angular momentum of two objects of roughly solar masses speeding around each other at relativistic velocity radiates away as gravitational waves. Correct?"

"Yes," Janeway said. "In theory."

"Then," Seven said, "as the orbit shrinks, the rate will pick up in inverse proportion to the fifth power of the separation between the two stars. It will be an immense quantity of energy. Am I correct?"

"Again, it would seem so," Janeway said, surpressing a smile.

"So you are proposing that we are to build a device that can intercept and store some of the gravitational energy that is being emitted from the neutron star binary?"

"To use it to help us get home," Janeway said.

B'Elanna frowned.

"In order to contain the immense amount of energy," Seven said, "within the confines of this device, we would need to distort the space-time continuum entirely out of shape inside the receptor."

"Theoretically, yes," Janeway said. "I can give you technical instructions based on the paper's theory. The original paper is stored in the ship's computer library."

"To be honest, Captain," B'Elanna said, "this sounds like a long shot."

By now Seven was so caught up in the hypothesis that she continued, ignoring Torres's reservations. "With such a virtually unlimited supply of energy, we should, theoretically, with certain modifications, be able to maintain a higher warp speed consistently, cutting many years from the length of the trip ahead."

Janeway nodded. "As well as supply our replication energy needs for a great length of time."

B'Elanna still wasn't convinced. "I don't see how we can connect the energy into the warp drives, let alone the ship's basic systems."

"A secondary concern," Seven said. Torres frowned. Janeway winced. If only Seven's tact were equal to her scientific acumen. "We must first gather and hold the energy before such a concern need be focused on."

B'Elanna actually snorted, but said nothing.

Seven turned to Janeway. "I trust you will want us to get started right away?"

"Yes," Janeway said. "I want us to be ready to start charging it up as soon after our arrival at the binary as possible. Our outside deadline, as I can figure, is that the device needs to become operational by the last day in the life of the binary. Theoretically, most of the gravitational energy will be radiated away during the last few hours, but we need the time to test the efficacy of the containment in advance. We ought to allow at least a few hours for that."

"Days, maybe weeks would be better," Torres said.

"I doubt we have that much time," Janeway said.

Both B'Elanna and Seven stood silently, clearly thinking about what she was asking of them. Finally B'Elanna sighed. "I suppose it's worth a try."

"At least," Seven said.

"I want this project kept secret from our Lekk visitors."

"Understood, Captain," Torres said.

Seven just frowned, as if telling anyone was the farthest thing from her mind.

"Keep me posted," Janeway said. She sat down behind her desk, glancing at the screen in front of her as her two officers left. She didn't dare let her hopes rise. That had happened too many times before. This idea was just another idea, nothing more.

"Report," Janeway said as she walked onto the bridge and headed for her command chair.

Chakotay stood and moved over. "Lieutenant Tyla is still in her quarters. She has made no real attempt to move around the ship, at least so far."

Janeway nodded. "Don't detain her if she tries. Just follow her. Also, let's find her something to do. Maybe help in the repairs of the yacht. Under strict supervision."

Chakotay smiled. "Understood." He turned to his comm link while she glanced around at Ensign Kim.

"How close are we, Ensign?"

"Two hours yet, Captain," Kim said.

She nodded. "Keep all sensors at full range. I want to know if there are any Qavok Empire ships anywhere near that binary."

"Understood," Kim said.

She stepped down beside her pilot. "Tom, when we get close I want to stop one million kilometers from the binary. No closer, at least not at first. We'll ease in later, if we can."

"Not a problem," he said.

She patted him on the shoulder and then dropped down into her chair, staring at the main screen, thinking about what was coming. Soon they would bear witness to one of the rarest natural shows in all the universe. And with luck, during the show they might even harvest some of the energy to help them get home.

If they could build the device to hold the energy.

If the Qavoks let them.

If the explosion itself didn't destroy them in the process.

Too damn many ifs.

Beside her was the empty spot where her coffee cup usually sat. She looked at it for a moment, then decided there was no point in waiting. It was time for another cup. She shoved herself out of her chair and headed for the door. "You have the bridge, Commander."

He smiled at her and nodded. He knew exactly where she was going. And she didn't care.

"Captain," Ensign Kim said, just as she reached the door.

She stopped and turned around. Her second-in-command was now no longer smiling, but instead staring at Kim's board.

"Lieutenant Tyla has escaped," Chakotay said. "Security reports that she has assaulted both of her guards."

"Are they okay?"

Chakotay nodded. "They're being treated by the Doctor."

"Use the ship's sensors to find her and beam her out of wherever she is hiding," Janeway said. "I'd suggest searching the shuttlebay area first."

Chakotay nodded and glanced down.

"Got her, Captain," Ensign Kim said.

"Good," Janeway said. "Just hold her in the transport buffer until I can get there."

Janeway strode to the turbolift. It looked like that cup of coffee was going to have to wait.

CHAPTER 5

TYLA'S PLAN HAD BEEN SIMPLE TO START WITH. GET away from the guards who were watching her room, then find one of these human's shuttles and take it home to warn her people. If she could fly a Qavok prince's yacht, she could fly a human shuttlecraft, she was sure. Even though the humans had beaten the Qavok easily, they didn't seem that much more advanced. And they were clearly not as military.

She eased closer to the door and listened, trying to make sure no one was in the hallway. She knew she was being guarded, even though she was sure Captain Janeway didn't want her to know. So her plan started as she simply went out for a short walk down the corridor.

She picked up a small statue of a creature she had never seen before. It was solid and had a hefty weight in her hand. It would do fine. She tucked it under her arm and stepped into the hallway.

As she had hoped, it was deserted, except for one of her guards, who was posing as an engineer working on a panel. She turned toward him, acting as if she knew exactly where she was going. And she did: off this ship.

She smiled and nodded to the guard.

The fool smiled back, then turned, pretending to get back to work. A half step beyond him she turned and knocked him out with the statue.

He went down with a soft thump.

She hoped she hadn't hit him too hard. There was no point in killing anyone. She quickly checked. He was still breathing, but she bet he'd have a hell of a headache in the morning.

She stepped back and around a corner as the other guard came down the hallway. He saw his companion and did what anyone would do, and what Tyla wanted him to do: he bent over to check the condition of his friend.

Tyla knocked him out, also, not as hard as the first one. The second guard went down with a grunt.

He'd have a headache too, she was sure.

Since she had planned her route before leaving her cabin, in less than a minute she was inside the shuttlebay. The human shuttle seemed small, and plain compared with the prince's yacht. It was square, with no real beauty to it. The door was open and she crawled inside, taking her time to study the instruments. She was sure she had a few minutes before the guards would be found, and then even longer before they thought to look here. She had time to make sure she didn't kill herself in this escape process.

Or at least she thought she did.

Suddenly the ship seemed to shimmer around her, and then it somehow vanished, as if it had been nothing more than a dream.

Then, without seeming reason, she found herself standing, facing a very angry Captain Janeway.

Beside her, guns drawn, were the two guards she had knocked out just a minute before, both not looking happy.

This wasn't possible. None of it was. How had she gotten here? She had been sitting a moment ago, now she was standing. How had the guards recovered so quickly?

None of this was possible. Yet to the captain, it all seemed normal.

"I'm waiting for an explanation," Janeway said.

Tyla glanced around, then stepped down toward the captain and the two guards. Forcing herself not to think about how the captain had pulled off such a trick, she faced the human woman. "Captain, I need to warn my people."

"Why?" Janeway asked, the sound of her voice

clear with anger. "Can they alter the path of a runaway neutron star, as you claim the Qavok can?"

"No, no," Tyla said. "But they can die trying to stop the Qavok. My people's leaders are hostages. We are at war." Why didn't this human see her point? It was so clear, so obvious.

"So you hit my people, attempt to steal from my ship, even though we helped you? And now we are in the process of rushing toward the neutron-star binary to stop the Qavok."

Tyla couldn't stand to look Captain Janeway in the eye. The truth of her words hurt, but she had done what she had needed to do. "Captain, I will do what I think is right to help my people."

Captain Janeway snorted. "You have a great deal to learn about helping anyone but yourself. Let alone what is right."

"But—"

Janeway waved her comment away. "Take her back to her room and make sure she stays there this time. Understand?"

"Yes, Captain," one guard said.

Janeway turned away, moving toward the door.

"Captain," Tyla said, forcing the shaking out of her voice to make it sound even more confident than she actually felt. "What would you have done in my place? You impound my ship, imprison me. What would you have done?"

Janeway stopped and turned. "I would have

spent a little more time understanding who was a friend, and who wasn't, before I took chances of making new enemies."

Tyla stood straight, shoulders back, and stared at Janeway. "You claim to be a friend of my people, yet I'm not free to go. Why?"

"At the moment, it's because you assaulted the two men standing beside you for no reason at all. They were not detaining you." Janeway stepped back toward Tyla. "Before that, it was because your ship was damaged and was not spaceworthy, and I didn't have the time to have my people fix it, considering that we might be going into a situation with the Qavok to save your entire home system."

"You make me sound ungrateful, Captain," Tyla said. Her words rang hollow in the small room. And instantly she wished she could take them back. For the first time she understood that she *had* been ungrateful. But the words were out there, and Captain Janeway was staring at her.

Finally, Janeway shook her head, spun on her heel, and left.

Tyla stood, staring, feeling the shock of being a fool. Finally the guard beside her nudged her gently with the point of his gun. "Let's go."

She glanced up at him, straight into his brown eyes.

"I'm sorry for hitting you," she said. She turned to look at the other guard. "And you, too."

The second guard nodded. "Apology accepted.

Now, please move forward, through the door and to the left."

She did as she was told, eyes down, thinking about what had been said. And knowing that she would try the same thing again if given the chance.

Janeway needed a moment to cool down. From experience, she knew that helping someone who was not grateful angered her more than it should. She made the choice to help others not for the reward, or for the thanks, but simply because it was the right thing to do.

But having someone like Tyla around didn't help her resolve, that was for sure.

She stopped just outside the engineering lab and took a long gulp of the warm coffee. It soothed her nerves a little, focused her on the important aspects of what was ahead: observing a dying neutron star binary, possibly getting energy for a faster trip home, and stopping a Qavok attempt to destroy another race. Tyla's concerns were not on that list at all.

She stepped toward the lab door and it opened. Inside, Torres and Seven were hard at work, side by side, both bent over the same panel. In front of them a part was being replicated, just shimmering into place.

B'Elanna heard the door open and turned. "Almost finished, Captain."

"There is little chance this will function," Seven

said, also straightening and turning to face Janeway.

"Why do you say that?" Janeway replied, moving to the panel and studying the work they had done on the energy-containment device. At first glance, it looked fine. Exactly what she had wanted.

"The energy will set up a standing wave pattern inside the container," Seven said. "It will rupture within three days' time."

Janeway glanced at Seven, then at the parameters for the container on the board.

"Not necessarily," Torres said wearily. Clearly the two of them had been arguing this point for the last hour. "Standing waves will form, but they can be broken regularly."

"Change the shape of the container," Janeway said, punching up her idea on the panel. After a moment she let the computer form a three-dimensional image of the new container, filled with energy. Then she set the image in motion. After a moment she nodded. "See? Let the waves break themselves apart."

Both Torres and Seven studied what she had done.

"It will take extra time," Seven said.

"It might work," Torres shot back, still studying the data.

"How long?" Janeway asked.

"Ten hours," Seven said.

"Do it," Janeway said. "I think we have the time. And keep me informed as to your progress."

"Understood," Seven said.

B'Elanna only nodded, clearly lost in the data on the panel.

Janeway started back toward the door, then stopped and turned. "Where is Dr. Maalot?"

"Engineering," Torres replied. "Since we needed this space for this project, I assigned him to help calibrate sensors."

"Any problems from him?"

B'Elanna looked puzzled. "None. He's like a kid with a new toy."

"He is overzealous," Seven said. "That is a dangerous trait."

Janeway smiled. "Noted."

She waited until she was out in the corridor before downing the last of her coffee. Even cold, it tasted wonderful.

CHAPTER
6

"PUT US IN A CIRCULAR ORBIT, MR. PARIS," JANEWAY said, dropping down into her command chair and staring at the sight ahead. "Keep a distance of one million kilometers."

"Yes, Captain." Paris's hands moved quickly over his console.

The neutron-star pair was a dizzying blur of two bright dots swirling around each other. Janeway had never seen anything move at such a speed, in such a tight orbit. The force at work in front of them was beyond comprehension. And *Voyager* was going to snuggle in real close to it all. Craziest thing they had done in a long, long time.

"All recording instruments on?"

"All working smoothly," Chakotay said.

Janeway nodded and sat back, staring at the incredible sight of two orbiting neutron stars. "Good. I don't want to miss a second of this."

"Captain," Ensign Kim said. "Dr. Maalot would like to talk to you."

Janeway tapped her combadge. "Yes, Doctor Maalot?"

"From my observations, the two stars are nearing the critical point. In about a day, I would say. We have arrived just in the nick of time."

"Perfect," Janeway said. "Everything ready and working there?"

"We are ready," Dr. Maalot said. He was beyond even trying to hide the excitement in his voice.

Janeway smiled. "Good. Keep on top of it."

She tapped her combadge again. "Seven, how are the preparations going?"

"Six hours and we will test the container."

"Understood," Janeway said, and smiled at Chakotay. Dr. Maalot's excitement was infectious, and she had to admit, this was exciting to her, also. She and the rest of the crew were going to be the first humans to witness an event like this. And witness it right up close and personal. She just hoped they got home with the data.

"Captain," Ensign Kim said. "There are two other ships holding positions close to the binary. They've just come into view."

"Where and who?" Janeway asked.

"Identity unknown," Kim said. "Both their orbits are circular with a virtually identical radius of about one hundred fifty thousand kilometers from the neutron stars."

"One hundred and fifty," Janeway said, almost whistling. "That's in there close. What about their orbital inclinations, Mr. Kim?"

"Effectively the same inclination as the double star's own orbital plane."

Janeway did a few quick calculations on her control panel, working to see if the two ship's orbits were safe or suicidal. After a minute she was sure they had picked the lowest safe orbit. But when the big event started, they were going to have to get out of there fast, or never leave.

"Mr. Paris," Janeway said. "Take us in. Circular orbit at a distance of one hundred fifty thousand kilometers from the binary. Match the inclination to those of the other two ships. I want to be within transporter range of the other two ships."

"Yes, Captain," Paris said, but he didn't sound happy about the order. He took a slow, deep breath and focused on his controls.

Janeway watched Paris for a moment, then glanced around at Tuvok. "Shields up. I don't want anything to take us by surprise here."

Tuvok nodded. "Screens up, Captain."

Paris was almost sweating as he focused on the controls in front of him. Taking a ship in that close to orbiting binary neutron stars made for tricky piloting, at best. Deadly, if done wrong.

"Ensign," she said. "Tell those other two ships we're coming in and that we're friendly."

"Understood," Kim said. "Hailing."

"Beautiful, isn't it," she said to Chakotay as the neutron stars grew in size, spinning around each other like two dogs chasing their tails.

"Amazing," Chakotay said. "Like ancient dancing gods, moving across the ballroom of the sky."

"You always did have a way with words," she said, smiling at him.

He only shrugged, never taking his gaze from the sight on the main screen.

Janeway tried not to hold her breath as she watched Paris take them slowly in, matching the speed and distance of the other two ships in a mad orbit around the two neutron stars. One slip and *Voyager* would be ripped apart by the intense tidal forces at work below them.

The process took less than a minute, but it seemed to go on forever.

"We're there," Paris finally said, after what seemed to be one of the longest silences Janeway could remember on the bridge.

Tom let out a deep breath and smiled at Janeway. Little beads of sweat covered his forehead and neck.

"Nice job, Tom," Janeway said. "Stand ready in case we have to make a quick escape. I want to be able to warp out of here almost instantly."

Paris nodded. "Will do."

Janeway stared at the incredible sight. In all her

years, she'd never seen anything like it. At this new distance, the ship traveled around the neutron star pair at a breathtaking rate of seventeen minutes per revolution, or at a velocity of almost a thousand kilometers a second. It was the only way the ship could hold against the incredible gravitational forces of the two neutron stars. They had to be traveling at a speed that would throw them away from any normal planet or sun, yet here they were held in orbit over the two neutron stars by the incredible gravitational forces at work.

The two other ships seemingly held positions stationary beside *Voyager* on the screen, even though they were moving as fast. The relative positions of the three ships remained virtually constant by their choice of similar orbital elements, a distance far enough to avoid most of the deadly tidal forces of the two neutron stars, but sufficiently close to enable the precise observations necessary for determining exactly when the moment of truth would arrive: the moment when the lesser of the two stars would explode and fling the primary away.

When that happened, Janeway wanted everything to be ready, and for *Voyager* to be a distance away. A long distance away.

"Any identity on the other two ships?" she asked, forcing herself to sit back in her chair and take a deep breath. "Any response?"

"No, Captain," Ensign Kim said. "One appears to be Qavok, but I'm not sure. The other, I have nothing to match it."

"Agreed, Captain," Tuvok said. "Second ship is of unknown configuration and armaments. I recommend caution."

"Screens are up, Mr. Tuvok," Janeway said. "But recommendation noted."

"Enlarge on screen," Chakotay said.

The images of the two ships filled the main screen, for the moment replacing the image of the binary. Janeway studied them. She had to admit that one of the alien ships had the primitive ruggedness of the Qavok frigate that they had rescued Tyla and Dr. Maalot from, except this one was substantially larger. Like the frigate, the ship had the outline of a misshapen ovoid with all sorts of protrusions. It reminded Janeway of pictures of a rhinoceros ready to charge. Ugly ship. Just plain ugly.

"Tuvok," Janeway said, "can you get a reading on strength of armaments and screens on that large ship?"

"It is the same as the other Qavok ship," Tuvok said after a moment. "It does not appear to present a real threat."

"Good," she said. "What about the other one?"

The second vessel looked eerie and almost ephemerally elegant beside the first. The exterior might have been conceived by a Rousseau or a Chagall. Although its shape did not really resemble it, the ship somehow evoked in Janeway's mind the image of Taj Mahal under a moonlit sky. The designer had a very strange vision as far as Janeway was concerned. Where she expected to see sharp, defined edges, she found only gentle curves. There were lines where no lines needed to be, portals where none seemed likely. Very strange, yet surrealistically appealing.

Both ships were similar in size, about on par with *Voyager*. And considering their location so close to the binary neutron stars, they were clearly shielded and powerful enough.

"Both ships are now hailing us, Captain," Kim said.

Janeway glanced around her bridge. It seemed that everything, at least for the moment, was on track.

"Set up a three-way conference, Mr. Kim. Make sure the other parties can see each other."

"Aye, Captain."

Janeway was not surprised to find a Qavok captain staring at her from the first screen, his reptilian teeth showing in what seemed to be a greeting.

The second screen showed a male face that looked almost human; perhaps these people were distant kin to the Lekks. Wide, green eyes and wide nostrils accented the thin face, making it seem more doll-like than anything else.

The Qavok spoke first. "I am Qados, captain of the Qavok Imperial Space Force warship *Invincible*."

Like Captain Qavim, this Qados was gruff and to

the point. Janeway instantly wondered why a warship was so close to the binary. A question she would get to later.

"Greetings," she said, nodding.

"I am Captain Fedr of the Xorm astrophysical survey ship *Gravity,*" the second captain said.

"Greetings to you, also, Captain," Janeway said. "I am Captain Janeway of the Federation starship *Voyager.*"

Captain Fedr bowed slightly.

Captain Qados made no move at all.

"I'm afraid, Captain Janeway, " Fedr said, "that I am not aware of a race such as yours in this area."

"Nor I," Qados said.

It was clear that Qados had not been informed from home yet about their rescue of the two Lekk escapees. She had no doubt he would be shortly.

"We are simply passing through this region," Janeway said, smiling. "Our primary objective is scientific exploration and an event like this could not be missed."

"It is special, isn't it?" Captain Fedr said, smiling. "A rare, rare opportunity for all concerned."

Captain Qados said nothing. She doubted, if there was truth to what the Lekks had told her, that he even cared about the science aspect of what was going on around him at all. He simply saw the phenomenon as a weapon, more than likely.

"I see that we are all here on an astrophysical expedition," Janeway said, glancing first at Chakotay to make sure he understood where she was going. "Why don't we bring our science officers into this conference at the beginning to make sure our communication lines in technical matters are open and uncluttered."

"Good idea," Captain Fedr said immediately, smiling. He looked sideways off the screen, then called out, "Dr. Janss, would you come and join us in this conference, please?"

Qados followed Fedr's move, then shook his head in near disgust. "Very well. If that is what you both want, give me a moment. I will summon Dr. Qentor, our senior science officer."

"I will need a minute, also," Janeway said.

She signaled Kim to cut the connection, then turned to Tuvok. "You up for playing science officer in this?"

Tuvok nodded. "I have a basic understanding of what is occurring with the binary neutron star. I should be able to, as humans say, fake it."

Janeway laughed. "Good. Because I can't spare B'Elanna or Seven at the moment. And I don't think our neighbors out there would like it if I played both parts."

"I assume you have a reason for this idea," Chakotay said.

"Just wanted to test their reactions," she said. "I'm surprised that the Qavok apparently have a science officer whose official functions are to conduct astrophysical research. I would not have expected as much from them, considering what the Lekks have told us they overheard."

Chakotay nodded.

"They may also be 'faking it,' Captain," Tuvok said.

"True," Janeway said. "Ready, Tuvok?"

"I am, Captain," he said, stepping down to stand beside her command chair.

Janeway signaled Kim that the connection should be opened.

Standing beside Captain Qados was another Qavok. "I am Dr. Qentor," he said.

"Dr. Janss," the Xorm standing beside Captain Fedr said.

"Tuvok," Tuvok said, bowing slightly in greeting. "According to our analysis of the preliminary data, the end to the life of this binary pulsar should come in a time span of about one day. Do you agree?"

Janeway wanted to smile at her security officer's opening. When you are playing from the weaker hand, play aggressively.

"That agrees with our predictions, from our initial observations," Dr. Janss said, nodding.

"Both your predictions basically agree with ours," Dr. Qentor said. "So, obviously you have analyzed the data properly."

"That's good to know," Janeway said, smiling.

"We are all here for a scientific quest," Captain Fedr said. "That much is clear. We all have the same objective—advancing our scientific knowledge. As it is, we are probably all a little short-handed and cannot do everything to our satisfaction. I suggest we help each other."

"And how might that be possible?" Janeway asked.

The Qavok captain seemed uncomfortable.

"If you two will agree, why don't we exchange a technical officer on a temporary basis? Possibly for only a few hours. For one thing, it will facilitate communications among our three ships. Working together we should be able to accomplish more. Gather more data," Fedr said.

Janeway was actually surprised at the suggestion. She wanted to find out if those two other ships were indeed here for their stated purposes and sending an observer to each alien ship would be a good way to accomplish that goal.

"I agree," she said. "A splendid idea, as long as the advisors have the ability to come and go as needed."

The Qavok captain appeared reluctant, and Janeway didn't blame him. They had put him in a terrible position. If his true mission here was to use the runaway neutron star as a massive weapon, hiding that fact from a trained observer would be difficult. Yet declining such an offer would also raise suspicions.

"We are perfectly capable of conducting our own research program," Captain Qados said, "without any help from either of you. But, if you both feel that you need help, I shall not begrudge it. I will agree to your proposal. As a favor."

Janeway smiled at the other two captains. "I'm sure Dr. Janss's team is also quite competent to carry out their objectives. As for *Voyager*'s astrophysical program, I have full confidence in our team's abilities. I've agreed with this proposal, however, because I do not wish to see any of us miss out on anything important."

"Granted, Captain," Captain Fedr said. "This is a once-in-a-lifetime event. Nothing should be missed."

Janeway noted that the Xorm captain didn't miss much at all, at least on the political side of things. She would not underestimate him, and she hoped to keep him squarely on her side.

"I told you already I was agreeing, didn't I?" Captain Qados said. "Let us proceed."

"I will need one hour to pick my two technicians," Janeway said.

"One hour it is," Captain Fedr said, and bowed slightly.

Captain Qados only cut the connection, leaving both the other captains smiling at each other before Janeway signaled to Kim that he should cut the communication link.

"Nice job, Tuvok."

"I did not do very much," Tuvok said flatly, moving back to his post at security.

"You did enough," she said, sitting back down

and staring at the beautiful, fast-moving neutron stars spinning outside. Just once she'd like to observe an event like this without the politics involved. Just once. Was that too much to ask?

She sighed. In this case it was.

She stood and turned to Chakotay. "Have Neelix meet me in my ready room in five minutes."

"Understood," Chakotay said.

She was almost off the bridge when the thought dawned on her and she turned back.

Chakotay was standing, facing her, smiling. "I'll have him bring a cup of coffee with him," he said.

"Thank you," she said. Then she laughed as she turned and went into her ready room. Five cups? Six cups? Who was counting?

"Sorry for the delay, Captain," Neelix said as he entered seven minutes later. "I had to brew another pot."

The wonderful, thick, rich smell of the coffee filled the room as he set the cup on the edge of her desk. It was as if she had been suddenly in a friendly kitchen, safe from the dangers of the universe around her. Steam drifted from the cup, beckoning her to take a sip.

She picked up the cup and held it under her nose, letting the smell and the heat fill her with strength.

"How much do we have left of the beans?"

Neelix shrugged. "Enough to last until Lieutenant Torres has time to replicate more."

Janeway only nodded. She very much hoped that

Neelix was right about that. She took another sip, then nodded to him. "Thank you."

"My pleasure, Captain," he said, smiling.

"So, I need what you know about the Qavok Empire, and the Xorm people."

"Xorm?" Neelix said. "We've met Xorm?"

"We have," Janeway said. "Is that bad?"

"I'm not sure," he said. "I've heard only legends, since my people never got to this area of space. They are concerned with science, art, and other pleasures of life."

"More advanced than the Qavok?"

"In some areas," Neelix said. "And clearly the Xorms are the more civilized of the two races. They have never used military conquests to further their needs. But they can defend themselves if pushed."

"So you think we might be able to trust them?"

"From what I know, I'd say we could, within their own rules."

"So, what do you think we can expect of the Qavok?" she asked, taking another sip of the wonderful coffee. The temperature had dropped just enough to make it perfect.

"The Qavoks are extremely warlike, with a cultural tradition that matches their outlook of the world. They cannot be trusted, Captain."

Janeway nodded. She already knew that.

"To a Qavok defeat is not an acceptable option— not at least from their official point of view. They tend not to fight if defeat is possible. They can be quite tricky."

"Somehow, that does not surprise me, Neelix," Janeway said, smiling at her friend.

"Anything more, Captain? I have some wonderful reeds simmering on the stove for stew."

"Just one more thing," Janeway said. "How about the Lekks? You know anything about them?"

"Very little," he said. "First I ever met were the two we had the lunch for."

"No general information," Janeway asked.

Neelix thought for a moment. "I have the impression that the Lekk are a strange people. A little backward, no real strong areas. I doubt if they've been around long. More than likely since the Qavok/Xorm alliance broke apart."

"Alliance?" Janeway said, putting her coffee down and staring at Neelix. Sometimes getting straight information out of the Talaxian could be so darned annoying.

"Oh, I'm sorry, Captain," Neelix said. "Their alliance broke apart centuries ago, and I felt it made no difference now."

"You know what happened?"

Neelix shrugged. "The history goes that the more warlike Qavoks broke away centuries ago to pursue a goal of building a galactic empire of their own. Since then the two races have been at odds with each other. But the Xorms know how to defend themselves and the Qavok haven't been able to make much headway. Must get under their skin." With that, Neelix grinned.

"So maybe this Lekk system is just a little trophy they're fighting over," Janeway said.

Neelix shrugged. "I can see no other reason for the Qavok to take it over. The Lekk systems offer them nothing."

"Nothing but systems to rule," Janeway said. "And some just want to rule for the sake of ruling."

Neelix nodded. "There is always that."

CHAPTER
7

"CAPTAIN," ENSIGN KIM SAID. "WE'VE GOT A problem."

Janeway pulled her gaze away from the hypnotizing effects of the revolving neutron stars and glanced around at Kim. The ensign had that worried look on his face he got every time trouble was headed their way. She had come to recognize it, and right now he was looking as worried as she had ever seen him look.

"Six Qavok warships are headed this way at top speed."

"Confirmed," Tuvok said. "Estimated time of arrival, two minutes, thirty-seven seconds."

"So much for our little scientific exchange program," Janeway said. "Mr. Paris, get us away from here. Put the binary between us and the approaching Qavok ships, then hold position. If we have to fight, I want to have some room."

"Understood," Paris said. His fingers flew over the panel in front of him.

On the main screen the images of the binary neutron star shrank. Janeway felt an odd sadness, as if she had been ordered to leave a friend. But at the moment she had no choice. There was no way she was going to ask Paris to hold an orbit close to two neutron stars while she fought with six ships. Too many chances for mistakes. But they would be back in time to watch the once-in-a-lifetime event from the perfect seat. She was going to see to that.

She stared at the screen for only a moment longer, then turned to Tuvok. "Are you monitoring Qados's ship?"

"I am," Tuvok said. "The *Invincible* has just gone to an alert status and powered weapons. They have not moved to follow us."

"And the *Gravity?*"

"The Xorm ship has raised its shields, but nothing more."

Janeway nodded. "The *Invincible* will follow the lead of the other Qavok ships. And we'll have seven against one. What are our chances?"

"Against all seven Qavok warships at once," Tuvok said, "we would have an approximate chance of survival of point one five, owing to the synergetic effect of their weapons."

"How about us against just two or three?"

Tuvok glanced at her. "Considerably better," he said.

She glanced at the screen. The neutron star binary was still centered there, the two stars circling each other only hundreds of kilometers apart but not quite touching. Of course, when one did touch the other, *Voyager* had better not be anywhere near here.

She punched the comm link for Engineering. "Dr. Maalot?"

A moment later the Lekk physicist said, "Yes, Captain."

"Do you have an estimated time remaining for the life of the binary?"

"About twelve hours," he said. "More than likely twelve. Why have we pulled away?"

"I'll explain shortly," she said. "Thank you."

She broke the connection and glanced at Chakotay. "Have Lieutenant Tyla brought to the bridge at once."

Chakotay looked puzzled.

"She might be able to help us against the Qavok. Her people have fought them before."

"Good thinking," Chakotay said, and turned to his comm panel.

Janeway stood and moved down beside Paris, staring at the binary on the main screen. She put her hand on his shoulder, feeling the strength under the fabric. "Tom, I want you to hold an orbit one million kilometers from the binary. When the Qavok fleet moves to come around at us, move away from them, keeping the same distance from the binary."

"Understood, Captain," he said. "But what if they split up?"

She patted his shoulder and moved back to her chair. "Now you're getting the idea. We want to make them split up."

"I see," Kim said. "They come from both the left and the right, we move down under. They send ships down after us, and we go up over the top. They have to keep a safe distance from the binary just as we do, so we use it to split them up."

"Exactly," Janeway said. "Improve the odds a little."

"Captain, that's an idea even Captain Proton would be proud of," Tom said.

"Well, thank you," Janeway said, then smiled. "I think. Ensign Kim, hail them."

"No response, Captain," Kim said after a very short pause.

"All ships have powered weapons," Tuvok said.

"It seems they want to fight," Janeway said. "Guess Captain Qavim didn't learn his lesson."

"Or he didn't tell them about it," Chakotay said.

"More than likely," Janeway said.

"Thirty seconds until the Qavok fleet will be within firing range," Tuvok said. "The *Invincible* has joined them."

"Tom," she said, "move us around the binary. Keep it between us and them."

The starfield beyond the binary shifted, moving on the main screen from left to right. She couldn't see the Qavok fleet of warships, since Tom was doing his job and keeping them on the other side of the binary.

"Three ships have split off and are moving to intercept," Kim said.

"Under them," Janeway said again, staring at the screen. "Make them split up again."

The silence on the bridge seemed to stretch and stretch.

Everyone did their job.

Janeway hated this part of any battle. It was when she could feel her nerves, when the coffee taste that had lingered in her mouth turned sour, when the pressure of her command chair under her seemed unbearable. She kept her attention focused on the screen and on Tom's fingers, as he moved them around the very dangerous binary neutron star. The only thing showing on the screen was the binary. No ship had managed to get close to them yet.

But she knew that would soon end.

"Hail from Captain Qados," Kim said.

"On screen," she said, standing.

The binary was replaced by the sneering lizard-face of Captain Qados.

"You run, Captain," he said. "Surrender now and you will not be harmed."

"And why should I surrender to you?" Janeway

said. "I have done nothing to harm the Qavok Empire. We have no desire to fight."

Qados laughed, or at least Janeway thought it was a laugh. "You harbor two Lekk thieves. And hold our prince's craft on your ship. Surrender now."

"We will gladly return your craft to you after the secondary star has exploded. The Lekk have asked for political asylum and I have granted it. We are here on scientific reasons." Janeway glared at the screen. "But we will not surrender."

"Then prepare to die," Qados said, and cut the transmission.

Janeway dropped back into her seat with a sigh.

"The guy can turn a cliché," Tom said.

"Three warships are in pursuit," Tuvok said.

"Good," Janeway said. "Ensign Kim, show a battle schematic of the locations of the seven Qavok warships, our position, and the binary."

"Yes, Captain," Kim said.

Janeway watched him as he worked furiously for a very long two seconds.

"On screen," he said without looking up.

She turned to stare at the battle schematic. It clearly showed all the Qavok warships with red dots and marked *Voyager*'s position with a blue dot. In the center of the image were small, circling binary stars. A green dot showed the location of the Xorm ship, very close in.

Two Qavok ships were bearing down on them

from the right, two from behind, one from the left, and two remained in position on the far side of the binary, blocking that route.

"Let's give them a little surprise," Janeway said. "Tom, reverse course hard. I want to go right through the center of those two pursuing ships. Forward shields on full, fire when in range."

"Aye, Captain," Tom said.

"Split screen, Ensign," Janeway said. "Half schematic, half forward images."

"Understood," Kim said.

The main screen split into two images. Schematic left, two Qavok warships on the right.

"Fire," Chakotay said.

Janeway sat, her hands gripping her chair as *Voyager*'s phasers made short work of the two Qavok warships.

It wasn't even really a fight.

The phasers sliced open the ships as if they were child's toys.

Not one shot from a Qavok warship was even fired, it all happened so fast.

"Two Qavok warships have been destroyed," Tuvok said.

"Have our odds improved?" Janeway asked.

"Considerably," Tuvok said.

"Good," she said. "Ensign, hail Captain Qados."

"Aye, Captain," Kim said. After a moment he said, "No response."

"Idiots," Janeway said, staring at the schematic.

The three ships had now formed one group and were in pursuit. The other two Qavok warships were moving to block their path.

She hated this situation. The Qavok were clearly outgunned and had no defense against *Voyager's* weapons. Yet the only way to prove it to them was to destroy ships and kill hapless Qavok warriors.

Stupid, stupid, stupid.

But Qados was giving her no choice in the matter.

"Mr. Paris, head right at the two blocking Qavok warships. Maybe if we take those two out, the others will pull back."

"Almost within firing range," Chakotay said.

"Fire when ready," she said.

She pushed her back against her captain's chair and watched as the blue dot showing *Voyager* bore down on the two red dots of the Qavok Empire.

"Firing," Chakotay said.

On the right side of the split screen two Qavok warships exploded as *Voyager* flashed past. On the left side of the screen two red dots vanished, leaving only three dots in pursuit.

"The two warships have been destroyed, Captain," Tuvok said, clearly stating the obvious. No damage to *Voyager*.

"Mr. Paris, keep us ahead of those others."

"No problem," Paris said.

Behind her the door to the bridge whisked open. She turned to see Lieutenant Tyla standing in front of two security guards, glaring at the screen. The red-haired Lekk was certainly a presence. She had on her officer's red cape, and the energy surrounding her seemed as defiant as before. It was an attitude that Janeway admired, even though it had already caused her more problems than she cared for.

"Join me, please," Janeway said, indicating that Tyla should move down in front of the screen beside her chair. Janeway indicated that the guards should remain near the door.

She waited until Tyla was beside her, then pointed to the left side of the main screen. "The three red dots indicate Qavok Empire warships."

Tyla seemed to pale, her already fine skin suddenly seeming pasty. "Captain, you must get away from here. Take me to my homeworld. We might be able to get enough reinforcements to beat them there."

Janeway managed not to smile, but Tom wasn't as tactful.

"Why?" he asked, glancing around at Tyla.

"Those are Qavok warships," Tyla said. "They will destroy you and any hope my people have of stopping this coming disaster."

Tom again laughed. "Two minutes ago there were seven of them."

"Your panel, mister," Janeway said.

Tom snapped back around, his shoulders squared.

"Seven?" Tyla asked. "You've destroyed four Qavok warships?"

It was clear to Janeway that the Lekk didn't believe such a thing possible. "We did," Janeway said. "I'm afraid a Qavok warship is no match for *Voyager.*"

Tyla's gaze turned from the main screen and held Janeway's. For the first time since Tyla had come aboard, Janeway could see the hatred in the Lekk's large green eyes turn off, replaced by respect.

And just a little bit of fear.

CHAPTER
8

WHEN LIEUTENANT TYLA HAD STEPPED FORWARD ONTO
the bridge of *Voyager,* she had been angry. The two
guards had offered her no explanation beyond the
fact that Captain Janeway wanted her on the bridge.
Being held prisoner by the humans was almost as
bad as being held by the Qavok. Only human food
was better.

The *Voyager* bridge was as impressive the second
time she stepped on it as it had been the first time
hours before. It was clean, well lit. Lekk warship
bridges were crowded, dark places, where the mood
seemed to always feel heavy and the underlying
smell was always of fear.

Lieutenant Paris, the man who had greeted her,
occupied a chair at a panel in front of the captain.

Beside Janeway sat Commander Chakotay, studying a small panel to his left. Others were at stations around the room. The main screen was cut in half, showing an image of the binary neutron star on one side and a schematic of a system on the other.

The two guards had eased Tyla into the room and the door had closed behind them, making her feel almost trapped. Captain Janeway had turned and seemed to study her for a moment, then motioned that she should come down to stand beside her chair. Tyla had done just that. Then the captain had told her that they were being chased by three Qavok warships, and Paris said they had already destroyed four.

For an instant, Tyla wouldn't believe that such a thing was possible. But then her inner voice, the voice she had trusted her entire life to steer her in the right direction, said that the captain and Lieutenant Paris were telling the truth. *Voyager* was much more powerful than any Qavok warship.

"So why do they continue to pursue us?" Captain Janeway asked. "You mentioned that defeat wasn't an option for the Qavok, yet Captain Qavim retreated. What exactly did you mean?"

Tyla glanced at the screen, then faced the human captain squarely. "I'm sure Captain Qavim is not alive, or he found another to take the blame. It is the way of the Qavok."

"For retreating?" Janeway asked.

"No," Tyla said. "For losing."

The captain still looked puzzled. How could she make the captain understand? "Let me put it this way," Tyla said. "There is no word for 'loss' in the Qavok language. They win or they die."

The human captain was nodding. "So we need to give those three ships a way out."

Now it was Tyla's turn to be confused. "Captain? A way out? If you can destroy them, you must destroy them. They are Qavok."

Captain Janeway gave her a sad but gentle smile. "It seems you are missing a few words from your language as well, such as 'compassion' and 'compromise.' "

Tyla could feel her face growing hot, her anger rising. She forced herself to stay still.

"I'm going to ask you to help me here," Janeway said.

Tyla took a deep breath and forced down her anger over the insult. "I will try."

"I'm going to ask you to give up your claim on the yacht, so I can return it to the Qavok."

"What?" Tyla almost shouted. Again she forced herself to remain still. She could see the two guards out of the corner of her eye. If she even made a wrong step they could cut her down instantly. "I suppose you would also like me to return to the Qavok?"

"Of course not," Janeway said. "But if we give them back the craft we might be able to stop the killing here. We'll drop you and Dr. Maalot off at your homeworld as soon as we witness the binary explosion. We have to stay here to make sure the Qavok don't send the unexploded star toward your homeworld."

Tyla forced herself to take another breath. The main screen still showed the three Qavok warships chasing after *Voyager* around the binary neutron star. It had taken a dozen of her people's ships to defeat three Qavok warships. Yet the craft she now was in could do it easily and didn't want to. Still they would make sure the Qavok did not destroy her homeworld. These humans were a very strange people.

"I relinquish my control of the yacht," Tyla said.

"Thank you," Janeway said, nodding. She had a faint smile on her face, as if she understood what Tyla was thinking. Could the humans also read minds?

"Hail the Qavok," Janeway said. "Tell them we'll give them what they want."

"Response coming in, Captain," the one they called Ensign Kim said.

"On screen," Janeway said as she stood. "Tyla, move sideways about two steps to get out of the picture. No point in rubbing salt in their wounds."

Tyla stepped sideways.

The face of a Qavok warrior filled the screen a moment later.

"You surrender?" the Qavok asked.

Tyla wanted to jump at the screen, scratch his tiny eyes from his face, stab the Qavok a hundred times in his dozen tiny hearts. Yet the humans around her seemed to have no reaction at all to the image of the Qavok.

Captain Janeway actually laughed at the Qavok. "Of course not. But I am willing to call a cease-fire. And to show my good intentions, I will return your prince's yacht to you."

"And the Lekk escapees?" the Qavok asked.

"They will remain on my ship and be returned home," Janeway said.

Tyla could hear the firmness in the captain's voice. The same firmness Tyla had felt when caught during her escape attempt.

"I will consider your offer," the Qavok said, and cut the connection.

In all her life, Tyla had never imagined a Qavok considering an offer of peace. Yet this human woman seemed to control them at her whim.

"Keep us ahead of that fleet, Tom," Captain Janeway said.

"No problem," he said. "As long as they stick together."

"I bet they will for the moment," the captain said.

"Confirmed," Tuvok said.

The captain turned to Tyla. "Any suggestions?"

"None," Tyla said, still staring at the screen in wonder.

"They had an alliance with the Xorm."

"That wasn't so much a peace treaty as it was a standoff."

"And that's lasted for thousands of years?" the captain asked, clearly amazed.

"That is what history teaches us," Tyla said. "I know nothing more."

Janeway nodded. "So it seems that if they don't take my offer, we're in for another fight."

Suddenly Tyla knew why the Qavok captain was acting the way he was. "Captain, under normal circumstances I do not believe the Qavok would take your offer. But by making it, you put the Qavok captain in a very difficult position."

"How?" Janeway asked.

"You are offering the prince's yacht," Tyla said. "If the Qavok captain turns you down and then destroys you, he also destroys the yacht and would, more than likely, be killed by the prince."

"But he can't really accept my offering because that would show weakness."

"Exactly," Tyla said. "More than likely they will accept your offer on the surface, then destroy you when they have the yacht."

"Try to destroy us," Janeway said. "They've already lost four warships."

"Yes, try," Tyla said, smiling.

Captain Janeway smiled back, and for the first time Tyla relaxed a little. Just a little.

"Qavok flagship hailing us," Ensign Kim said.

"On screen," Janeway said, again motioning that Tyla move back a step or so.

Tyla quickly did so as the ugly face of Captain

Qados appeared, larger than life on the large main screen.

"Captain," he said. "I will accept your offer."

"Fine," Janeway said. "Here are my terms."

"Terms?" the Qavok almost roared. "I did not agree to terms."

"You want your prince's yacht, you will agree to these," Janeway said, smiling.

Tyla wanted to laugh as Janeway made Captain Qados fume for a few seconds before going on.

"First," Janeway said, "two of your ships must move at least one astronomical unit away and hold position until the secondary star explodes."

Tyla watched as the Qavok captain said nothing.

"Second," Janeway said, "we will drop the prince's yacht exactly one hour after the secondary has exploded at a location of my choice, a safe distance from the explosion. You can pick it up there."

"No!" the Qavok shouted.

Tyla had never seen a Qavok actually flustered. He looked almost humorous as his scales seemed to push away from his hide. His mouth flapped open and closed and his eyes watered.

"Too bad," Janeway said, dropping back down into her captain's chair.

Tyla was amazed how relaxed she looked.

"Destroy me," Janeway said, "and you destroy the prince's yacht. I doubt he's going to like that very much, now, do you? Especially since by simply waiting some twelve hours, you can return it to him safely."

Again Tyla watched as the Qavok's mouth opened and closed. His scales flapped as if a strong wind were moving them. Finally he said, "I agree. All but the *Invincible* will move off to a holding position."

"Good," Janeway said. "Now we can get back to studying this binary neutron star."

Tyla thought she heard the Qavok captain snort in disgust before the connection was broken.

"This is a first," she said.

"Two of the warships are breaking orbit and moving off," Ensign Kim said.

"Keep an eye on them, Mr. Tuvok," the captain said.

"I will do just that, Captain," Tuvok said.

Tyla felt like rejoicing. In all her life she never would have imagined that one ship could back down three Qavok warships, yet she had just watched it happen.

Captain Janeway wasn't even smiling.

"You won, Captain."

Janeway shook her head. "I think the war is far from over. The real first is going to happen before us in the next few hours. And I would still wager Captain Qados and the *Invincible* are going to try something."

Tyla felt her stomach twist. "You mean like sending one of those neutron stars toward my homeworld?"

"Maybe," Janeway said, staring at the image of

the neutron star binary on her screen. "Or maybe something else. I honestly don't know."

Tyla glanced at the screen, then back at Janeway, realizing that she had just witnessed something else for the first time. A captain actually admitting a weakness. It didn't happen in the Lekk fleet and she doubted it did in the Qavok fleet. These humans really were strange beings, of that there was no doubt. Very strange indeed.

CHAPTER

9

IN ALL HIS LIFE DR. MAALOT COULD NOT HAVE IMAG-
ined a ship like *Voyager* And being on such a ship,
watching the final hours of a binary neutron star,
was not even something he could have dreamed.
The entire last day had seemed unreal, as if maybe
he had actually died on that small yacht and this
was an afterworld of some sort.

He finished calibrating the sensor and glanced
around the area called "Engineering." A dozen
humans, both male and female, worked silently at
panels, or over instruments, as he was doing. The
area was big and well lit, and felt, for lack of a
better term, scientific. It was cleaner than any lab at
home, as if ready for inspection by top government
officials. Only here, in Engineering, this was how

things always were. Everything in its place and a place for everything. He had never seen another lab like it before.

A half-dozen humans worked silently while the large bluish column in the center seemed to pulse lightly, making no real noise. All seemed well, normal.

He glanced down at the panel near him. It showed the details of the binary with incredible accuracy. From the readings, there wasn't much time left before the two would touch, in a virtual sense, causing the distended secondary to explode and sending the more massive primary shooting through space, the deadliest missile ever conceived by the universe. In about ten hours.

His finger flew over the board, bringing up a schematic showing the plane of the two neutron stars' orbits. Then he extended that plane like a flat board through the nearby star systems. The plane cut the Lekk system like a knife. If the Qavok succeeded in sending the runaway neutron star at his homeworld, or even close to it, there would be nothing left for him to return to. If that happened, he had already decided to ask if he could stay on board.

Behind him the door swished open. Maalot turned and smiled as Captain Janeway entered. She returned his smile, seemingly at ease. That surprised him. She had just come from standing off Qavok warships, yet she looked as if the incident had been an everyday occurrence. Maybe for this ship it was.

"Doctor Maalot," the captain said, "are you ready?"

"Just finished the last sensor," he said. "We'll get readings on every band, in every spectrum of light and gravitational radiation, from all angles. We'll have so much information, we could almost rebuild the binary."

"Wonderful," Janeway said, laughing. "But I think once is enough for me."

"Agreed," he said, laughing with her.

"We're almost back in position," she said. She glanced down at the schematic he had displayed on the board, then up at him.

Her gaze held his, and he could feel the understanding coming from her. "We won't let the Qavok destroy your home," she said, her voice firm.

"Thank you" was all he could think to say.

She moved so that she stood directly over the board. Her powerful hands didn't move as she studied something. And after a moment her shoulders slumped. She turned to him. The expression on her face had changed from a smile of elation to a frown of worry.

"Doctor, I need you in the briefing room in ten minutes."

He nodded. He couldn't think of anything to say. What had caused her sudden shift of mood?

As one accustomed to having her orders obeyed without question, she turned and headed for the door. He watched her for a moment, then turned back to the schematic displayed on the control panel.

What could have caused such a reaction? Had he done something wrong?

For the next five minutes he studied the schematic, finding nothing. Then, after getting quick directions from a crew member, he headed out for the briefing room. It was the longest two-minute walk he could remember taking.

She was the first in the conference room, and she allowed herself to drop down into her chair for a moment. It had taken her only a minute to get the information she needed from the prince's yacht's computers. Far quicker than she had expected. She tried to make herself sit back, relax a little. This was clearly becoming one very long day. She had already had four cups of coffee. Or had that been five? She'd lost count. But she'd also lost count of how long she'd been awake now.

She sat back, forcing herself to take a deep breath and relax her tight muscles. She could feel the joints cracking in her back as she moved her shoulders around. She would have time to rest later. In just a few hours, one of the rarest events in the galaxy would take place. And she was going to be there, watching, maybe even helping it along a little.

The door from the bridge opened and Chakotay

entered. He smiled at her and moved around the table while others filed in behind him.

"Status of the Qavok, Mr. Tuvok?" Janeway asked as her top staff, as well as Lieutenant Tyla and Dr. Maalot, filed in and took seats around the conference table. Only Paris and Neelix were missing. The two Lekk guests looked nervous. Dr. Maalot's hands were shaking and he was sweating. Tyla, on the other hand, showed her nervousness by holding her shoulders tight, in a formal posture. Her straight gaze never wavered.

"The two warships have taken up a position one astronomical unit away," Tuvok said. "They have been joined by two more. It would be logical to assume more will join those. The *Invincible* has returned to its original position."

Janeway nodded. "Captain Qados is rebuilding his fleet."

"It would seem that way," Tuvok said.

Janeway shrugged. "Fine by me, as long as they stay right where they are until we get our explosion. Have we taken up our strategic orbit around the binary?"

"We have," Chakotay said. "Tom is staying at the helm to make sure nothing goes wrong. Screens are up."

"Good," Janeway said, nodding to her second-in-command. She too felt better with Tom at the controls. He was by far the best pilot they had, and if something happened with the binary, she wanted him at the controls.

She glanced at Torres and Seven. "Is your project finished?"

"Within the hour," Torres answered.

"We should be working on it now," Seven said, clearly annoyed at the interruption.

"In a moment, Seven," Janeway said, holding up her hand for Seven to stop. "This won't take long."

Seven said nothing, but Chakotay looked puzzled.

Janeway sighed softly. She would tell him what was going on as soon as the meeting was finished. She had planned to brief him before now, but just hadn't had the time.

The door swished open and Mr. Neelix entered. "Sorry I'm late, Captain," he said, smiling at her as he slid a cup of coffee beside her on the conference table.

"Thank you, Neelix," she said, letting the cup sit. At the moment she had to deal with the problem she had discovered.

"Dr. Maalot," she said, "in Engineering you had a schematic showing the orbital plane of the neutron-star binary. All the possible paths the larger neutron star will take after the explosion."

"I did," he said.

"Would you be so kind as to put that on the main screen so we can all see it? B'Elanna, please show Dr. Maalot how to do that."

It took only a moment before the image was in front of all of them.

"Tyla and Dr. Maalot believe that the Qavok will

attempt to send the star at their home system. Right?"

Both Tyla and Dr. Maalot nodded.

"It is what we overheard," Tyla said. "We would not lie about such a thing."

Dr. Maalot was again nodding.

Janeway held up her hand. "I'm not saying you lied. I'm just trying to get the facts in front of all of us here."

Tyla said nothing, so Janeway went on. "B'Elanna, on the screen show the area on both sides of the Lekk home system that the star must pass for the Qavok to be successful. Say one thousand astronomical units on either side would do the damage."

"I doubt our system would remain intact at that range," Dr. Maalot said.

"I agree," Janeway said. "But we need to draw the line somewhere."

Two short parallel lines appeared on both sides of the Lekk system on the schematic.

"Now," Janeway said, "extend those lines so that they go off the chart on the edge."

B'Elanna did as she was told.

Janeway barely avoided wincing when she saw an area they had cut out of the schematic.

"Before the meeting I downloaded the records of inhabited worlds in this area from the prince's yacht," Janeway said.

With a few quick keystrokes she overlaid the

inhabited systems in the area on the schematic, showing the inhabited worlds as green dots.

"Many of those worlds are primitive at best," Tyla said. "I don't see their danger to the Qavok."

Janeway glanced around at her staff. All of them, it seemed, were seeing what she had seen in Engineering. "B'Elanna, show the orbital plane as a two-thousand-astronomical-unit-thick disk."

The engineer nodded, and a moment later the schematic on the main screen changed to show a volume of possible destruction.

"Oh, my," Neelix said softly.

Janeway knew exactly what he meant. They were inside a star cluster, and there were a few dozen systems within this volume at danger from the runaway neutron star. Why hadn't she realized this before now? And now that she had, what could they do about it?

If anything.

"Captain," Torres said. "It's even worse than it seems."

Janeway focused on her chief engineer. The half-Klingon was clearly shaken.

"I took this possible path here," B'Elanna said, "and extended it."

A silence filled the room as if someone had died. Finally Torres said, "It extends through the heart of the Federation and the Alpha Quadrant."

"What?" Chakotay said. "Are you sure?"

She nodded. "There is as much a chance of the

runaway neutron star plowing a path through the Federation as there is of it taking out the Lekk homeworld. Of course, it will take time for it to get there, but it will get there. Actually, predicting its exact course over such a long path is tricky because of the differential galactic rotation and close encounter with stars that could deflect the trajectory."

Again silence filled the room as they all tried to absorb what Torres had just said. Janeway was having her own problem with it. She had become so used to their own distance from home, she was having a hard time understanding that an event they were witnessing could destroy entire systems in the Alpha Quadrant. That just didn't seem possible.

Yet she knew it was.

She forced herself not to think about the possible destruction. It was up to them to make sure it didn't happen.

"Okay, people," she said. "What are we going to do about this?"

"Changing the timing of an exploding neutron star is not possible," Seven said.

"One optimistic nonsolution," Janeway said. "Anyone else?"

No one said a word.

"B'Elanna, on the schematic eliminate any path that would cause destruction to an inhabited system, either here or in another part of the galaxy."

B'Elanna nodded and bent over the panel in front of her. On the schematic, section after section disappeared, as if some person were eating slices of the pie one large piece at a time. Finally there was only a small slice of the pie left. A very small slice.

"If the runaway takes this path," B'Elanna said, "it will miss all systems and leave the plane of the galaxy eventually."

Janeway looked at that small area. How in the world were they going to control one of the rarest and most powerful events in nature, enough to send a neutron star along that path?

It didn't seem possible.

But it had to be possible. Otherwise they were about to witness the death of entire systems full of beings. And that wasn't an option.

"Dr. Maalot," she said. "How much time do we have?"

Maalot shrugged. "The separation between the two neutron stars is under seven hundred kilometers now, and the revolutionary period of the two has decreased to under a half a second." He seemed to think for a moment, then went on. "Eight hours. "I'd count on the eight hours."

"I want ideas in front of me in one hour," Janeway said, her voice as firm as she could make it. "Dismissed."

She sat and studied the schematic as her crew stood and, without saying a word, filed out of the room. Then, as the door whooshed closed, she picked up her cup of coffee and sipped it, letting the wonderful flavor clear her mind.

There had to be a way to send this neutron-star monster out into empty space between the galaxies.

She took another sip and then stood. A few hours before, she had been as excited as a child to be able to watch the coming explosion of a neutron-star binary. Now she was calling it a monster.

Typical of this galaxy. The most beautiful things were often the most deadly. You just never knew.

She headed for her office, cup in hand. She had work to do, a solution to find.

If there was a solution.

CHAPTER
10

SEVEN WAS BENT OVER AN ENGINEERING PANEL WHEN Janeway entered. As was typical, Seven didn't look up or even acknowledge that anyone else was in the room, even though Janeway knew that Seven was very aware of everything that went on around her. She just chose not to react to most of it. Janeway often wished she had the same option and control.

On the monitor above the panel was the clear image of the revolving neutron stars. They now were so close, and moving so fast, they looked indistinguishable from each other. Faint whiffs of hot plasma were drifting away from the spinning pair along their equatorial plane. Janeway had gotten to the point over the last forty-five minutes that she didn't want to look at the binary anymore. Yet its deadly beauty kept drawing her to watch it.

"Any ideas?" Janeway asked, taking her gaze off the monitor and moving up beside Seven to see what she was working on.

"If you refer to a solution to directing the neutron star's path, I do not believe a solution is possible. So I have finished the gravitational wave energy containment and tested it. It works within acceptable parameters."

At first Janeway wanted to shout at Seven for disobeying her order to work on finding a solution. But she managed to keep her mouth shut as Seven turned back to the panel. Seven, actually, had been obeying orders. It was clear she had worked on the first problem for as long as it took to find the answer—that there was no solution. Then she had continued with Janeway's first order, to construct an energy containment to harness some of the intense gravitational energy pouring off the neutron star binary in its final hours of life.

Janeway forced herself to take a deep breath and remember why she had come here to talk to Seven in the first place. She had wanted to run some numbers past her, to confirm her own findings.

"Seven," Janeway said.

Seven turned back to face her.

"Let's just say," Janeway said, turning and pacing, "that an explosion set off at the appropriate time and spot could quicken the timing of the explosion. Would it be possible to time that explosion in such a way as to direct the runaway neutron star?"

"Theoretically, yes," Seven said.

Janeway nodded. "I came to the same conclusion. And obviously so did the Qavok. But what size explosion would be needed? That's where I got stumped."

"I did not," Seven said, "as you put it, get stumped." She keyed in a few numbers on the console and nodded for Janeway to look.

Janeway could feel her stomach clamping up. That number was even bigger than the one she had first come up with. It would take an extremely powerful explosion to cause any change at all in the neutron binary's normal course of dying. More firepower than all their phaser and torpedo power focused on one spot at the same instant. Twenty times as much, at least.

For the first time in a long time, Janeway felt small in comparison with the universe around her. When she'd first gone into space, she'd had that feeling often. But over the last few years they had beaten so many things that she hadn't really been overwhelmed by the universe in some time.

Until this moment.

Outside the ship an event was unfolding that would most likely destroy entire planetary systems and send out enough energy in one huge burst to power all the Federation ships for thousands of years.

What made her think she could alter such a thing? How had she been so arrogant?

"I ran a warp-core-breach scenario," Seven said, her fingers flying over the keyboard. She motioned for Janeway to read the calculations on the screen. "Breaching *Voyager*'s core against the puffy secondary might provide the energy barely sufficient to change the timing of explosion."

It took a moment for Janeway to fully understand what Seven had suggested and then discarded as not feasible. She had run, as if it were a matter of course, a suicide option for the entire ship. And was now reporting it as if it were just another daily log entry.

"Therefore," Seven went on, "we are not capable of changing the binary's disruption, so I completed the energy containment as you requested. It is now collecting and functioning within acceptable parameters."

Janeway glanced up at the monitor, at the rapidly revolving neutron stars, but not yet touching. "There has to be a way," Janeway said. "We can't just let those worlds die."

"There is no choice," Seven said, turning to go back to work.

Janeway shook her head slowly from side to side, as if shaking Seven's words from her ears. "There has to be a choice," she said. "I won't accept anything else."

With that she spun and headed toward the door,

her stride firm, her resolve set. She would find a way, if it meant breaking every rule of nature and physics.

Tyla stood beside the Vulcan Tuvok on the bridge as the captain returned. Janeway had asked her if she was going to try to escape again. When Tyla had said no, where would she go with a fleet of Qavok warships standing guard nearby, Janeway had dismissed the two guards and had told her to help Tuvok where he needed it.

So far, the security officer had not needed her help, or even spoken to her. Yet Tyla was determined to follow the captain's orders and help where she could.

Dr. Maalot had been given a station beside Mr. Kim and was humming softly to himself as he worked gathering data from the neutron-star binary that filled the main screen. He didn't seem to be worried at all about the outcome of the events around him, but instead was focused completely on the death of the binary. Tyla envied his focus. Her focus was on saving her people and there was nothing she could do toward that goal at the moment.

It was a hopeless feeling. A feeling she was not used to.

"Lieutenant Tyla," Janeway said, smiling at her. "Join me for a moment. You too, Dr. Maalot."

"Gladly, Captain," Maalot said.

Tyla said nothing as she stepped away from Tuvok to follow.

Janeway also nodded for Commander Chakotay to follow her and then led the way through a door off the bridge.

After a moment Tyla found herself in what was clearly the captain's personal office. It had a warm feel, yet was very neat and completely functional. Tyla decided it fit Janeway's personality perfectly.

Janeway was already sitting behind the full-sized desk, when the door slid closed behind Chakotay and Dr. Maalot.

She looked up, first at Tyla, then at her second-in-command. "We're running into a problem here," Janeway said. "Our calculations show that it would take a massive explosion, timed perfectly, to send the binary into its last stage and control the flight of the runaway star."

Tyla understood what Janeway had said. It was the Qavok plan to destroy her homeworld. Dr. Maalot was also nodding.

"Our problem," Janeway said, going on quickly, "is that we don't have enough power on this ship to cause a large enough explosion. Not even close."

"What?" Tyla asked, unable to remain silent. "This ship is far more powerful than a Qavok warship. You've proven that. How can you not have enough power when they do?"

"That is exactly my question," Janeway said.

"Either we're missing something in our calculations, or the Qavok have miscalculated and will fail in their attempt."

"Captain," Dr. Maalot said, "may I see your calculations?"

"Of course," Janeway said. With a few taps on her pad, she swung a small screen around on her desk so Dr. Maalot could study it.

Tyla glanced at Chakotay, who stood silently, waiting. Janeway watched Dr. Maalot go over the numbers, her expression passionless, almost cold. Tyla managed to force herself to also remain calm. Yet as each moment ticked by, she felt as if the last hope for her people was fading. She knew that was just her imagination, and she tried to ignore it. But she was a trained fighter. Standing and watching someone else do the fighting was not in her nature.

Finally, Dr. Maalot glanced up at the captain. "I'd like to run more calculations," he said. "But on the surface, your calculations seem correct."

"So is it possible," Janeway asked, looking directly at Tyla, "that the Qavok have some sort of special weapon or explosive capabilities we don't know about?"

"How large?" Tyla asked.

"Large enough to shatter a small planet," Dr. Maalot said.

Tyla actually laughed before she could catch herself. "If the Qavok had such a weapon, do you think they would use it in such an indirect way?"

She stared at the captain, making sure her point

went clearly home. "If the Qavok had such a weapon, they would have long since used it against my planet. So the answer to your question is no. The Qavok do not possess such an explosive force."

Janeway nodded. "So they have either miscalculated, or they have figured another way of affecting the path the neutron star will take. And that's what we've got to find out quickly."

The captain turned to her second-in-command. "I want you to run any scan you can think on the Qavok warship *Invincible*. I want anything unusual pinpointed on that ship."

"Understood," Chakotay said.

"Dr. Maalot," Janeway said, "I'd like you to run calculations to confirm our findings as quickly as possible, then I'd like you to search for any possible way to alter the secondary's explosion with less power."

"I will do that, Captain."

"Good. Lieutenant Tyla, you go with Commander Chakotay. I assume you know the basic layout of a Qavok warship."

"I do, Captain," Tyla said.

"Good," Janeway said. "So if you two find something different over there in your scans, I want to know about it."

Tyla nodded. For the first time since *Voyager* had saved them, she felt like she had a useful task to perform.

"We're going to make Captain Qados mad,"

Chakotay said, smiling. "I doubt their screens will block our scans."

"Good," Janeway said. "Let him take a shot at us and we'll end this quickly."

Tyla wanted to rejoice. Finally, the captain had the attitude she had hoped for.

"Will do," Chakotay said.

"Dismissed," Janeway said. She swung the small screen on her desk around and began to study it.

Tyla followed Chakotay out of the room.

This was too good to be true. Let Dr. Maalot study his stupid stars. For her it was far, far more important to study a Qavok warship.

And then live to get the information home.

CHAPTER
11

JANEWAY FINISHED GOING OVER THE CALCULATIONS one last time. The energy needed to cause the secondary star to explode at an exact moment was far, far too immense to even consider. Yet she knew, without a doubt, that they were missing something.

She pushed herself away from her desk and checked the time. About eight hours from now, the secondary neutron star would lose too much mass to maintain its nuclear degeneracy, causing a massive explosion that would send the more massive neutron star hurtling through space, the deadliest missile ever conceived by Mother Nature.

Janeway was making no progress at all. Maybe someone else was. It was time to check.

Finishing the last sip of her coffee, she headed onto the bridge. Chakotay and Lieutenant Tyla were hunched over a sensor panel. Dr. Maalot and Ensign Kim worked silently in the communications area. Tom worked the controls, keeping *Voyager* steady against the increasingly rough gravitational forces coming off the neutron star binary.

"Anything, Commander?" she asked as she moved up behind Tyla.

"Nothing," he said.

Tyla nodded, the frustration clear on her pale face and wide, green eyes.

"As far as we can tell," Chakotay said, "the *Invincible* is a standard Qavok warship. Except for an unusually large crew, nothing extra has been added or removed."

"Then they seem to think," Janeway said, "that a regular phaser shot that wouldn't even cut through our shields will change that binary's death course?"

Chakotay nodded. "It would sure seem that way. Unless they've discarded the idea of trying it."

"If they had done that," Tyla said, "the *Invincible* would not be in this position. They do not care about scientific data. Unless it can be used as a weapon."

Janeway tended to agree with Tyla on that count. "Okay, then we're down to two options on this track. Either the Qavok calculations are so far off as to be laughable, or they have figured out another way."

"They are warriors, Captain," Tyla said. "Not bright, but clearly not stupid. I'm sure they think their method will work. And I would not bet against it."

"Okay, so we need to find what they have found. You two keep searching."

"And annoying Qados in the process," Chakotay said, with a barely perceptible grin.

Tyla seemed pleased with that notion, also.

"Good," Janeway said. "Keep scanning him."

"Will do," Chakotay said.

Janeway turned and glanced at Tuvok. "How many now in the Qavok fleet?"

"Three more warships have been added, bringing the total to seven holding one astronomical unit away."

Janeway shook her head. Captain Qados was about as obvious as they came. "Keep an eye on them."

"Captain?" Dr. Maalot said.

Janeway moved over between him and Ensign Kim. "Tell me you've found something."

"I just might have," he said. His fingers flew over the board in front of him. He was amazingly adept for someone who had only seen the system for the first time a few hours earlier. He pointed to the screen.

An illustration came up. It was a chart showing energy and results. Energy expended on the x axis, amount of motion resulted on the *y* axis. A simple diagram.

Dr. Maalot pointed to a peak area of motion. "We started with a desired result and worked backward," he said. "So we got a fantastic energy requirement for a result."

He tapped the board and another diagram filled the screen. Same layout, but different line in the center.

"I plugged in the energy output of one of *Voyager*'s phaser beams set on continuous fire, then plotted the result on the neutron star binary."

"And?" Janeway said, still not catching the exact meaning of the chart on the screen.

"If you had fired one phaser at the bloated secondary neutron star six days ago and kept it up for three hours, against the star's rotation, it would have changed the final outcome of the explosion by exactly six-tenths of one millisecond."

Janeway looked at the Lekk physicist. He was beaming at his discovery. She didn't follow.

"Doctor," she said, "we weren't here six days ago. We only have a few hours. What can we do?"

"I don't know exactly," he said. "But don't you see? It's figuratively like using a fulcrum on a large rock. It takes so much energy to move a rock directly. It takes less when using a fulcrum. I've just found one fulcrum to move the secondary neutron star. There will be others, I'm sure, if we open our minds and think outside the desired result."

Janeway stared at the diagram on the screen and

suddenly knew exactly what he was talking about. They had been asking for a result and working backward. They needed to research different methods and look at the outcome.

She tapped her combadge. "Janeway to Torres and Seven."

"Go ahead, Captain," B'Elanna said.

"Yes?" Seven said.

"I'd like you both in my ready room in five minutes."

"Understood," B'Elanna said.

"Someone must monitor our experiment," Seven said.

Janeway smiled. "Can you rig up a sensor to allow you to move around the ship and still monitor it?"

"I can do that," Seven said. "Five minutes."

"Good," Janeway said. "Out."

"Doctor," she said to Maalot, "would you join us in my ready room in five minutes." He nodded at the request.

She was almost back to the door into her ready room when Ensign Kim stopped her.

"Captain, the Xorm ship is hailing us."

Janeway shook her head. In the fight with the Qavok and all the push to solve the problem of directing the neutron star so it wouldn't destroy entire systems, she had forgotten about the Xorm ship.

"On screen," she said, moving over and standing in front of her command chair.

Captain Fedr's face appeared. He was smiling, still wearing the same garments he'd worn earlier.

"Nice fighting, Captain," he said, almost laughing. "The Qavok do not take easily to defeat."

"I've heard that," Janeway said. "And if they'd just left us alone, they wouldn't have lost those ships."

"I know that," he said. "You seem to be an honorable race, you humans."

"We do our best," Janeway said.

"I'd like to warn you about something we've heard," Captain Fedr said.

"Well, thank you," Janeway said.

Fedr shrugged. "Anyone who can set the Qavok on their heels as you did deserves all the help they can get."

"So what have you heard?" Janeway said. She really didn't have time to stand here and gossip. There was too much work to do and not enough time to do it.

Captain Fedr took a deep breath and dove right in. "The Qavok intend to try to alter the course of the larger neutron star. I know that sounds impossible, but they seem to think they can do it. We're not exactly sure where they plan on trying to aim the thing."

Janeway nodded. "We've heard the same thing. But we are at a loss as to how they intend to do it."

"As are we," Captain Fedr said, almost relieved that Janeway knew about the Qavok plot. "The energy needed would be too extreme for them to produce."

"We've come to the same conclusion," Janeway said. "But what worries me is that they believe they can do it. They must have run the same mathematical calculations as we did."

"True," Fedr said. He was now frowning. "Very true. The Qavok are not entirely stupid."

"My people are working on the problem now," Janeway said. "If we discover anything, we will let you know at once."

"And we will do the same in return," Fedr said. "Good luck."

"And to you," Janeway said.

Captain Fedr's face was replaced by the images of the revolving neutron stars. She stared at it for a moment, just taking in the incredible beauty of it. And the magnitude.

It was Dr. Maalot who set the tone for the meeting with a provocative question.

"Seven," he said, "if a warp core were dumped into the neutron star, what would be the result?"

"The tidal forces would tear it apart, causing a breach and a warp-core explosion."

"And would such an explosion have an effect on the less massive of the neutron stars?"

"Of course," Seven said. "But the energy would not be enough to cause the explosion at an exact point in time."

"Not at the exact *moment* of the warp-core explosion," Dr. Maalot said. "But it would alter the eventual time of the final moment of the binary, and thus alter the course of the neutron star runaway. Am I correct?"

Seven stared at him for a moment, then said, "You are correct."

"So," B'Elanna said, slowly. "If we know the exact time of the coming explosion and then work backward, we should be able to find a point where applying enough energy would change that time enough to cause a desired change of path for the runaway star."

"Exactly," Dr. Maalot said.

"That would not be practical to predict," Seven said.

Dr. Maalot ignored her. "The two stars are orbiting each other every few hundred milliseconds at the moment. Even the slightest change in the equilibrium of the secondary could cause it to explode sooner."

"Very true," Janeway said. She glanced at B'Elanna. From the look on her face, it was clear the chief engineer was following Dr. Maalot.

"It is not possible to predict the exact moment of the secondary's explosion," Seven said.

"Who says?" Janeway asked.

Seven looked at Janeway with surprise etched on her determined face. "I have assimilated hundreds of different races. They all believe it would not be possible."

"I don't care," Janeway said. "I want you to run computer models on that binary. We've assumed up until now we couldn't predict it. Well, I'd like to try."

"I will try," Seven said, nodding.

"Good," Janeway said. She knew without a doubt that Seven's try would be the best any of them could do, and then some.

CHAPTER

12

"SIX HOURS, THIRTY-SEVEN MINUTES, EIGHTEEN SEC-
onds, twenty-one milliseconds, two hundred nine
microseconds," B'Elanna said. "I agree with
Seven."

B'Elanna, Seven, and Dr. Maalot were standing
with Janeway in the astrometrics lab. On the display was a section of space near their present
location. Hundreds of stars seemed to float in the
air in front of them, like fireflies. Seven had marked
the inhabited systems in a green tint. It gave the
display an almost festive feel, if not for the line
cutting through the entire area.

A death line as far as Janeway was concerned.
Seven had put a red-tinted cylinder around the

line showing the deadly area of a one-thousand-astronomical-unit radius. Janeway had no doubt the radius was bigger than that, but for now that line and red-tinted cylinder were enough.

And it would all start in six hours and thirty-seven minutes.

If Seven's calculations were correct, the larger neutron star would destroy three inhabited systems on that path, and who knew how many more beyond this area of space. Three green lights were inside that red-tinted area.

And once the neutron star started on that path, there would be nothing anyone could do to stop it.

"If my calculations are short by one millisecond," Seven said, "this would be the path." Seven keyed in a number and the line and red cylinder shifted slightly to Janeway's right.

Janeway studied it for a moment. On this line only two inhabited systems would be destroyed. One millisecond to save millions of lives. It seemed so harsh.

"If my calculations have allowed one millisecond too many, this would be the path." The line shifted quickly back to the left. Again three inhabited systems would be destroyed.

Three different systems.

"I've checked your computer model," B'Elanna said. "I'd bet on your hitting the time right on the money, within a fraction of a millisecond at most."

Seven nodded and said nothing.

"So how much of a shift are the Qavok trying

for," Janeway asked, "if they plan to send the star at the Lekk system?"

Dr. Maalot started and Janeway touched his arm as a way of apology. She knew he must have family, friends there. If the Qavok succeeded, there would be time to evacuate the entire system, but it would still mean the loss of his homeworld.

Seven did a few quick calculations, then keyed in her findings on the astronomical display floating in front of them. The stars shifted and the line snapped to the left, cutting through the center of the Lekk system. "The explosion of the secondary neutron star must be sped up by two point four one milliseconds to get this path."

"I agree," B'Elanna said after a moment. "I figured the same result."

Janeway nodded. She didn't want to leave anything to chance; that was why she had both Seven and B'Elanna doing calculations. A very tiny mistake now would mean disaster to millions later.

"We can't let them do that," Dr. Maalot said.

"Don't worry," Janeway said assuringly. "We'll stop them."

Maalot nodded and took a deep breath. Clearly seeing the line run through his home system had shaken him. It would have shaken her if that line had gone through Earth. But Janeway was even more afraid of the next question, afraid to ask it, to find out that what she asked was impossible.

She glanced at the display, then turned to face Seven. "How much must the final explosion be shifted to send the star safely out of the galaxy?"

Seven did another adjustment to the display and again it shifted. Only this time there were no green-colored stars anywhere inside the red-tinted cylinder of death.

"The final explosion must happen two point three nine milliseconds earlier than predicted," Seven said. "To do so, we must increase the mass loss from the secondary star at this exact time."

Janeway nodded. A huge amount of time considering the forces at work. But just maybe it would be possible.

"Agreed," B'Elanna said.

Seven nodded at her.

Beside them Dr. Maalot was doing fast calculations. After a moment he looked up, beaming. "If the mass loss is increased by point zero one six percent, the explosion will come exactly three point one five milliseconds earlier.

"How much energy would be needed to do that?" Janeway asked.

Dr. Maalot, B'Elanna, and Seven all worked at the calculation. Janeway stared at the line moving safely past all the inhabited systems. If there was a chance of making this flight path for the neutron star happen, they would take it.

Dr. Maalot finally broke the silence. "The amount of energy I came up with is staggering."

"The exact same amount as a warp-core breach," Seven said. "Within acceptable and controllable parameters."

Janeway stared at Seven for a moment. She had been afraid that would be the answer. This wasn't a situation she wanted to be put in. But she knew math doesn't lie.

"So," B'Elanna said, "the energy would be almost the same to move the star at the Lekk system. Right?"

"Yes," Seven said.

Dr. Maalot just nodded.

"So where do the Qavok think they are going to get a warp-core breach?"

Silence filled the room as all of them thought about B'Elanna's question. Janeway didn't much like what she was thinking. Because if Captain Qados was planning to dive his ship into that binary, she was going to have to destroy him first. And she didn't like that idea at all.

"I'm fairly certain that Qavok do not commit suicide," Dr. Maalot said. "Especially by the shipload."

"Yes, but would they die for their cause?" B'Elanna asked. "Like good soldiers?"

Janeway glanced up at the display. The path of the neutron star went harmlessly out of the galaxy. No inhabited systems were destroyed. It was the only option they had. They had to try for it, somehow, some way. Doing nothing cost too many lives.

"How long until we have to send a warp core into that star to get this scenario?"

Seven and B'Elanna both set quickly to work.

After less than ten seconds Seven looked up. "Five hours, twenty-three minutes, ten seconds, fifty-nine milliseconds."

Torres looked up and nodded.

"All right," Janeway said. "I want a countdown. Have the computer remind us every thirty minutes that we've got that long to find a way to send a warp-core-sized explosion down into that binary. And stop the Qavok from doing the same. Let's get to work."

Janeway spun and left the lab, headed for the bridge. If an answer could be found, the three of them would find it.

She would come back and keep them moving shortly. But right now there were two things she had to check on before she could make the next move. Something that Chakotay had said nagged at her.

And something that Tuvok had said.

"Five hours, twenty minutes remaining."

The computer announced the time to the entire ship just as Janeway walked onto the bridge. The entire bridge crew looked puzzled. She imagined that most everyone on the ship did too. But they would soon be filled in on the details.

"Listen up, people," Janeway said as she stepped down and stood beside her command chair. "This is how long we have to find a way to send the big neutron star below us on a safe path out of this galaxy. One millisecond later and entire inhabited systems will die."

The silence on the bridge was heavy.

Chakotay simply stared at her.

Ensign Kim's mouth was slightly open.

Beside her Tom was shaking his head from side to side in clear disbelief.

"So everyone stay sharp," she said. "We won't have a second chance at this."

She stepped up to where Chakotay and Lieutenant Tyla were standing. "Anything more?"

"Nothing, Captain," Chakotay said.

Tyla's large green eyes were intense, but Janeway could tell that she was disappointed also.

"Does the *Invincible* have a second warp core on board?" she asked. "A shuttle, or an experiment of some sort?"

"No," Tyla said. "Qavok warships do not have shuttles with warp drives. Their shuttles are used mainly for ship-to-ground movement. Or ship-to-ship. Simple ion-propulsion drives only."

"No extra warp core found in our scans," Chakotay said.

Janeway nodded. She was afraid of that. She went on to the next question. "You mentioned that there were extra Qavok crew members on board the *Invincible?*"

"That's right," Tyla said. "The normal crew for a warship is one hundred and sixteen. There are one hundred and forty-six on that ship. An extra thirty crew members."

"Why?" Janeway asked. "Can you see any reason?"

"None," Chakotay said. "They seemed to be doing nothing at all."

Tyla nodded. "They are bunched in what seems to be a hangar bay, as if they were simply passengers."

Suddenly Tyla's face paled even more and her wide green eyes turned to slits. "Or an attack force."

"What?" Janeway asked.

Tyla faced her. "Quvok elite fighting companies consist of exactly thirty soldiers. Thirty is an important number to them; it has some religious significance. Why didn't I see that before now?"

"You saw it now," Janeway said. "That explains a great deal, actually."

"How?" Chakotay asked.

Janeway held up her hand. "I've got two more questions to find answers to before I try to answer that."

Chakotay nodded as Janeway faced Tyla. "To your knowledge, would the Qavok ever sacrifice an entire ship to accomplish a mission?"

Tyla shook her head. "Not if they didn't have to. They are not a self-sacrificing people, Captain."

"Okay," Janeway said. "That takes care of that option."

She turned to Tuvok. "Have more Qavok warships joined the group yet?"

"No. The count remains at seven."

"And don't you think that they arrived there fairly quickly?"

"They were clearly close by, Captain," Tuvok said.

"And having that many warships close by is logical to you?"

"Not at all," Tuvok said. His gaze held hers for a moment before he went on. "Clearly they had planned to be in this area for some reason not related to our presence."

"My thought exactly," Janeway said. "And we spoiled their plan in some fashion or another."

Janeway turned back to Chakotay, then decided to tell the entire bridge crew. "All right, everyone, here's what is happening."

She waited a moment until everyone had glanced up at her, then went on. "We've discovered that it would take a warp-core-breach level of energy to alter slightly the timing of the coming neutron-star explosion. And that warp-core breach must be timed perfectly."

Around *Voyager*'s bridge her crew nodded. Lieutenant Tyla looked intense.

"We've also tracked the path the primary neutron star will take after the explosion of the secondary one. It will destroy three inhabited systems in the next few centuries. So, as I said earlier, we're going to try to change that path. That's why the countdown."

Paris was nodding. Tuvok had one eyebrow raised in thought.

"We also believe that the Qavok are going to try to alter the path of the neutron star to pass through the Lekk system, among others. We don't know where they're going to get an extra warp core, but I have no doubt they will."

"The troops," Tyla said. "They plan on invading the Xorm ship and using it."

"Possibly," Janeway said. "But that's only one possibility. We need to attack this on two fronts. First, we stop the Qavok. Second, we set up a change of our own. Everyone follow what's happening?"

"Got it, Captain," Paris said. "Except where are we going to get an extra core?"

Janeway paused for a moment, knowing how Tom was going to take this news. He invested his heart and his soul in the new shuttle. "We'll have to use the shuttle."

He glanced around at her, a stunned look in his eyes.

"We'll build another one," she said.

All he did was nod, then turned back to his controls. But then, before she could say anything, he spun back.

"Hey, what about the prince's yacht?"

Janeway looked at his face, then laughed. "I promised to return it to them."

"If they held off until after the neutron star explosion," Kim said. "From what you just said, it doesn't look as if they will do that."

"Very good point," Janeway said. "And if they do attack in any fashion, either us, or the Xorm ship, or try to change the neutron star explosion, we'll use their yacht. All right?"

"All right," Paris said. He seemed even more pleased with himself than usual.

"Your controls, mister," she said.

Paris spun around, still smiling.

"Tuvok, I want long-range sensor scans of the surrounding area."

"Understood, Captain," Tuvok said.

"Lieutenant," she said, speaking to Tyla, "would you mind helping B'Elanna make sure the Qavok yacht is ready to go?"

"It would be my pleasure," she said, smiling. Her wide-set green eyes seemed to almost glow.

"I'll tell her you're coming," she said. With a few quick steps she was off the bridge and into her office. She found herself smiling, also glad that they wouldn't lose their new shuttle. Using the Qavok prince's yacht had a nice feel to it.

Sort of poetic justice.

CHAPTER
13

TYLA GLANCED AROUND AT THE PLUSH FURNISHINGS OF
the yacht. The perfumed air seemed thick in comparison to *Voyager*'s clear, odorless atmosphere.
The carpet made the floor feel spongy under her
feet, and the mood lighting seemed far, far too low
to ever work in.

It now felt like a decade since she and Dr. Maalot
had frantically climbed aboard this small ship. The
five minutes it had taken her to familiarize herself
with the controls were the longest five minutes she
had ever lived. But she had been lucky. No Qavok
had noticed them boarding the yacht. She had
gotten the five minutes she needed.

Pure luck. Nothing more.

And they had been lucky to have *Voyager* come

to their rescue. She was still embarrassed at her fruitless escape attempt from *Voyager*, but no one had said a word about it since. And now she felt she was being trusted. Humans were a very forgiving species. She would not have done the same in Captain Janeway's place.

"Grab the edge of the panel," B'Elanna said.

Tyla snapped back to her present job. She and B'Elanna had to get the yacht up to flying just far enough to get down into the clutches of the neutron star binary. And do it at just the exact moment.

Tyla lifted the panel away and B'Elanna stuck her head into the compartment behind it. It was a service hatch for the engine room of the ship. There was no real door into that room.

"Bring those tools," B'Elanna said, pointing to some equipment on the deck. Then she turned and crawled inside the opening, standing up in the small room on the other side.

Tyla followed quickly, also standing.

The inside of the engine room was strikingly different from the luxuriously furnished main cabins of the yacht. It was hidden from view of the prince, as if seeing it might harm his delicate sensibilities. If a Qavok had delicate sensibilities.

The deck was bare metal; the walls were, likewise, plain metal sheets. The room smelled faintly of burnt circuits. Not a good omen, Tyla guessed.

B'Elanna flipped open a sensor and began taking

readings. After a moment she shook her head. "The warp core is still active, but we'll be lucky to get this thing to fly even on thrusters."

"What can I do?" Tyla asked.

"How much engineering experience do you have?"

"Not much," Tyla said. "But I know ships."

B'Elanna nodded. "See if you can run some diagnostics on the ship's systems. I'll start by getting the thrusters back on-line."

Tyla nodded. "I'll be at the controls. Yell if you need my help."

"Will do," B'Elanna said, sounding distracted. Apparently she had already shifted her focus to the task that faced her.

Tyla crawled out of the engine room and back into the plush furnishing of the main cabin. After a moment she was back in the pilot's chair, isolated in the small area off the front of the main cabin. The seat felt comfortable to her.

The thought made her shudder.

That flight from the Qavok system was the longest she ever remembered. And she had spent practically every minute of it in this chair. And she had been prepared to die in this chair.

Her fingers danced over the familiar control board, and after a moment she had diagnostic programs running on the warp core, thrusters, and shields. It would take a few minutes for the runs to finish.

She sat back and let her mind drift. She had sat like this during those hours of flight. Alone in here, with Dr. Maalot pacing in the main cabin, not knowing if she would be blown out of space at any moment.

Waiting.

Fearing.

The small pilot area suddenly felt smaller and smaller, as if the walls were closing in around her.

She had to escape, to push the craft harder and harder.

She had no choice.

The walls closed in even more.

"Relax," she said aloud, her words echoing in the cabin. Through the port she could see the interior of the *Voyager* bay.

"You're safe," she said aloud, just to hear her own voice and force the images away. "Breathe." She forced herself to take a deep breath.

That helped. The walls stopped closing in.

She took another deep breath and the panic slowly ebbed, leaving only the nagging fear that something was wrong.

But nothing was at the moment.

It was going to be very nice to watch this yacht explode in a neutron star.

She'd never have to see it again, sit in this seat again, remember those hours of panicked flight again.

She just might cheer.

* * *

Dr. Maalot glanced over at the half-Borg, half-human named Seven. She stood over a panel, working intently. The woman was a wonder. Logical, extremely smart, and cold as the outside of an interstellar freighter. He'd met many aliens in his time, but never one like her.

He moved over beside her and glanced at the board. She seemed to be running a diagnostic on a storage container. Some sort of energy-storage unit. Gravitational in nature. But before he could see any more she shut the program down and turned to him.

"Have you completed your calculations?"

"I have," he said. "They agree with yours to the tenth decimal point of a second."

"Good," she said. "You will help me."

She turned back to her board and keyed in another program.

"With what?" he asked.

"We must determine exactly how long the yacht will remain intact descending into the tidal forces of the neutron star binary."

He glanced at the board where she'd been running the diagnostic. "Do you mind telling me what you were running the diagnostic on?" he asked.

"I mind," Seven said, her voice flat and without emotion. "We must complete our calculations."

"You are quite the slave master," he said, shaking his head.

"I do not consider you a slave," she said. "Nor

am I your master. We have our orders. Nothing more."

Dr. Maalot held up his hand for her to stop. "Tell me what you want me to do."

Seven nodded and pulled up the numbers they would start with, including the basic structural integrity and shield strengths of the yacht. He watched, wondering how anyone on *Voyager* ever managed to talk to Seven. Or if she even had a friend. From his experience with her, he'd guess she didn't.

And he doubted if she missed it.

"Four hours and twenty minutes remaining," the computer said as Janeway dropped down into her command chair. On the main screen the binary had become a blur of the two neutron stars chasing around each other. Wisps of plasma seemed to be escaping the intense gravitational fields as the two stars tore at each other like street fighters trying to knock each other down. In this case, the primary, which was actually smaller in size, would win. And very soon.

And they only had four hours and twenty minutes before they would attempt to change the time of that final battle between the two neutron stars. Change it by two point three nine milliseconds.

Four hours and twenty minutes. Not much time to attempt the impossible.

Janeway wondered what those in command back

on Earth would think of this. By moving the star's path, she was more than likely violating the Prime Directive. Cultures that would be destroyed would now live, if she was successful. And some might interpret stopping the Qavok from taking their yacht back as a violation of the Prime Directive as well.

Just one violation right after another.

But it was far, far too late now to back out. What was the old Earth saying? "In for a penny, in for a pound." At this point she was working on her first ton.

"Mr. Kim," she said, "hail Captain Fedr on the Xorm ship. It's time to have a little talk."

"Aye, Captain," Kim said.

She watched the incredible sight of the binary for a moment before Kim said, "On screen, Captain."

"Captain Fedr," she said as the wide-eyed face of the Xorm appeared. "Thank you for responding."

He smiled, his green eyes almost sparkling with excitement. "At a time like this, it is a pleasure. Life is a pleasure when witnessing a wonder of the galaxy."

"I wish I could say the same for us here," Janeway said.

Her words wiped the smile right off his face. His eyes became intense and very focused.

"Is there a problem?" he asked.

"If you don't mind, I'd like to take the long way to that answer," Janeway said, and she proceeded to explain her crew's findings.

"Core breach?" Captain Fedr echoed as she finished. He looked over at his colleague, Dr. Janss, who only nodded, lost in thought and calculations.

Captain Fedr didn't seem to much like the thought of a core breach. He had probably had a few close calls in his past. Just about any starship captain had.

"Captain," Janeway said. "The Qavok may be trying to use the same idea we've discovered to alter the path of the star to take it across the Lekk system."

Captain Fedr nodded. "So there actually might be a way for them to succeed. We had written off that rumor as impossible."

"Not impossible," Janeway said. "A core breach aimed at another point of the less massive and larger neutron star eighty-one minutes before the projected time would cause it to hasten the time of explosion by two point four one milliseconds."

"And that would do it?" Dr. Janss asked.

Janeway nodded. "I'll be glad to send you our calculations."

"I would love to see them," Dr. Janss said.

Janeway glanced around to Chakotay, who was standing over a panel near Tuvok. "Send them to him."

"Working on it now," Chakotay said.

"But Captain," Fedr asked, "do you know how the Qavok intend to accomplish this feat?"

"Not exactly," Janeway said. "But I do have a theory."

"Which involves us?"

"It might," Janeway said. "We've been intensely scanning the Qavok warship for the past few hours. They do not have an extra warp core on board in any fashion."

"That's not surprising," Captain Fedr replied.

"But they do have an extra thirty crew members, standing by in a large group in one of the shuttle-bays."

"You said thirty?" Captain Fedr said, his face growing slightly pale and his eyes closing down to narrow slits.

Janeway nodded. "Thirty. We think it is one of their elite fighting forces."

"The Qborne," Fedr said. "The most dreaded name in the Qavok military. They always travel in units of thirty."

Janeway waited a moment for Captain Fedr to collect his thoughts, and then she said, "We think they are possibly on board to take over your ship and use your warp core to alter the neutron star."

"They wouldn't dare," Captain Fedr said, red-ness slowly filling the pale skin under his green eyes. "We haven't had such an act of aggression between our two races for hundreds of years."

"Well," Janeway said. "I felt I needed to warn you and your crew, so that you might get ready.

We'll be glad to help you if such an attempt is made."

"If what you say is true, we could use all the help we can get," Fedr said. "We are outfitted as a research craft. We would stand no chance against the Qborne."

"Fine," Janeway said. "Consider us your protector until we need to get out of here ahead of the explosion. After that, you're on your own."

Captain Fedr actually smiled again. "Thank you, Captain Janeway." He started to cut the connection when Dr. Janss said something from off screen.

"Oh, Captain," Fedr said, "my chief physicist wants to know if you are going to try to alter the course of the neutron star yourself. And if so, how?"

Janeway laughed. "If we think it will work, and save those inhabited systems, we're going to try. Right now our plan is to use the warp core on the Qavok prince's yacht."

Captain Fedr stared at her for a moment; then he burst into laughter.

"Captain," he said between chuckles, "I like you more and more every minute."

"Same here," Janeway said, finding herself almost laughing along with the Xorm. "I will be in touch."

She motioned for Harry to cut the connection, and then she turned around.

Her entire bridge crew was smiling, except, of course, Tuvok.

"He's got quite a laugh," Harry said.

"Infectious," Chakotay said.

"That it is," Janeway said, still fighting not to burst out laughing. "That it is."

CHAPTER
14

"THREE HOURS AND FIFTY MINUTES REMAINING," THE computer said as the last of the senior officers filed into the meeting room.

Janeway was privately beginning to regret having ordered the countdown. Whenever the computer reminded them of the time, the knot in her stomach twisted again, pulling at her insides like a monster eating at her. They had to find a way to solve this.

She forced herself to try to relax as she waited until everyone was settled. Everyone was present except Tom—who was remaining in the pilot's chair until this was all over—and the two Lekk passengers. Janeway had excluded them because she had wanted only crew in this meeting, so they could speak as freely as possible.

"Reports?" she said.

B'Elanna shifted forward on her chair. She had a black smudge on her cheek and another on her shoulder. "The yacht has more problems than I care to count," she said. "Bad design, bad construction, and really bad maintenance, for starters. But the good news is that the warp core is intact and functioning. I think I can get their ion drive up and running enough to fly the thing down into the star."

"Shields?" Janeway asked.

"Never had much to begin with, but what it had is there and operating. One of the only things that is. I can install enough shields to last as long as we need them to."

"Good," Janeway said. Then she turned to Seven expectantly.

"The yacht's warp core is insufficient to cause the desired results we need to effect a change in the explosion of the secondary neutron star."

"What?" Janeway said, rocking back as if the news had just slapped her.

And in a way it had.

She had been counting on using that yacht.

"Please explain," Chakotay asked.

"The warp core of the Qavok yacht," Seven said, "is approximately four times smaller than our main warp core on *Voyager*. The resulting explosion—when the tidal forces of the binary breach the core—will not be sufficient to change the time of the final binary disruption by two point three nine milliseconds."

Seven sat there, impassionately, seeming to wait for the next question. But Janeway didn't know what the next question was.

"How short will we be?" Chakotay asked.

"Short enough to send the star through five inhabited systems," Seven said, "and solidly into the Alpha Quadrant many millennia in the future."

"There's no way that is going to happen," Janeway said.

Chakotay leaned forward. "What about the shuttle's warp core? Is it any larger?"

"Only slightly," Seven said. "Not enough." Seven seemed to pause for a moment, then said to Janeway, "But if I may mention the containment project, I might have a solution."

"Go ahead," Janeway said. She had almost completely forgotten about that project. The idea of hitching a ride home paled in comparison to stopping the destruction of inhabited star systems. It was a similar decision to the one that had brought them to this quadrant in the first place.

A decision she had finally come to grips with.

"We have collected," Seven said, "a significant amount of gravitational wave energy in a containment field. The original intent was to use the energy, if we could capture it, to speed our trip home. Am I correct, Captain?"

"You are," Janeway said.

"And it's stable?" B'Elanna asked. "I've been too busy to even check it."

"I've watched it closely," Seven said. "It is stable."

"So what is your solution?" Janeway asked.

"A concentrated blast of the energy stored in that container, measured carefully and focused at the same instant and point in space as the yacht's warp-core breach, would provide sufficient energy to hasten the explosion of the secondary neutron star."

Janeway tried to imagine how that would work. How would they fire the energy? How would they measure it? They had barely figured out a way to contain it safely, let alone use it so quickly.

"There are drawbacks to this plan," Seven said.

"I can think of a good dozen right off the top of my head," B'Elanna said, worry creasing her features. "But give me yours first."

"I think most problems might be solved in the short time allotted," Seven said, staring at B'Elanna. Then she turned to Janeway and continued. "However, *Voyager* would have to be in a much lower orbit than we are in now for this plan to work effectively."

"Lower?" Janeway asked.

Seven nodded.

"I can hear Tom screaming from here," Chakotay said.

No one laughed.

"How much lower?" Ensign Kim asked. "Tom's sweating just trying to maintain this orbit."

Seven glanced at Torres, then back at Janeway. "We would have to follow the yacht down to two thousand kilometers above it when our bombs explode."

"We would not survive that," B'Elanna growled, starting up out of the chair at Seven.

"Easy, B'Elanna," Chakotay said, putting his hand on her arm to settle her back into the chair.

Janeway also motioned for her to keep calm, but she knew Torres was right. She doubted they would survive a warp-core breach at that distance, let alone under those tidal forces. Plus there was a good chance that if they were that close to the binary, they would not be able to climb away fast enough, out of the neutron star's gravity well, even under *Voyager's* full power.

"I said there were problems," Seven said.

"You weren't kidding," B'Elanna grumbled. "You just didn't say the problems would be terminal."

Seven did not reply.

Janeway sat back in her chair and glanced around the table, the knot in her stomach tighter than it was when they had started the meeting.

Chakotay glanced at her. He too looked worried.

It was time she set something straight.

"Just to clear the air here," she said, still leaning

back in her chair, pretending to remain as relaxed as possible. "I have no intention of destroying this ship to change the path of that neutron star. Do I make myself clear?"

There were a few nods around the room.

"Good," she said. "That bloated secondary is going to explode very shortly. As I said before, if we can find a way to change the runaway's path, we will. Otherwise, we record the event, take what energy we can from it, and then move on."

Those words sounded cold to her ears, but she knew her crew needed to hear them.

She needed to hear them.

"Seven," she said, "you and Dr. Maalot continue to work on your calculations. Find a way to direct more narrowly that gravitational wave energy from a greater distance."

"That will not be possible."

"Make it possible," Janeway said. Then she turned to B'Elanna. "You and Lieutenant Tyla continue getting the yacht ready. If we can find a solution to this, I want to be prepared."

"Understood," B'Elanna said.

"Captain," Ensign Kim said. "I have an idea that might work."

"Go ahead," Janeway said.

"Would it be possible to connect the shuttle and the yacht with a tractor beam and rupture both cores at the same instant?"

Janeway glanced at Torres.

"It's possible," the engineer replied.

"And maybe add in some extra explosives," Kim went on, "like storing the gravitational wave energy container in the shuttle, to add a little extra boost to the explosion?"

B'Elanna shrugged. "Again, that would be possible."

"Seven," Janeway said, "you and Dr. Maalot do the calculations for the scenario that Ensign Kim just outlined. See if that would be enough."

"Yes, Captain," Seven said.

"Any of you," Janeway said. "If you have an idea here, don't hesitate to tell me. We're not going to solve this one by going by the book."

"The book went out the window a few light-years back," Chakotay said, smiling.

"That it did," Janeway said. "I want updates in one hour. Dismissed."

Six minutes after the next computer warning— "Three hours and twenty minutes remaining"— Tuvok called for her.

"Captain to the bridge, please."

She was beside him in less than ten seconds.

"The thirty Qavok aboard the *Invincible* are moving, Captain," Tuvok said. "They seem to be boarding a vessel in a shuttlebay."

Janeway stared at the readings. It was clear they were moving, but how long would it be until they attacked? And exactly where would that attack be?

"One more thing, Captain," Tuvok said. "Four

more Qavok warships have joined the seven standing off one astronomical unit away."

"How fast can they get here?"

"Two hours, ten seconds," Tuvok said.

Janeway nodded. "Then we'll probably have just that much warning."

"That would be logical," Tuvok said.

Janeway didn't want a fight, but it seemed the Qavok had other ideas. If it wasn't one damn thing, it was another.

She turned to Ensign Kim. "Hail the Xorm."

"Aye, Captain."

She stepped down beside her command chair as Captain Fedr's face filled the screen.

"The Qborne seem to be boarding some vessel," Janeway said.

Fedr's face paled, and he nodded. "Thank you for the warning."

"We think they will attack at approximately the same moment that their other warships arrive. That will give us about twenty-two minutes' warning."

"We see they've been gaining strength," Fedr said. "We've put in an emergency call to our homeworld, but there are no other ships close enough to help us in time."

"Well then," Janeway said, "it looks like it's just the two of us. They won't know what hit them."

"I hope you are right," Captain Fedr said, smiling.

But Janeway could tell he was only smiling on the surface.

"We'll continue monitoring their activity," Janeway said, "and warn you the moment we see something."

"We will do the same," Captain Fedr said.

"Good," Janeway said. "And one more thing. You mind if I toss a little scare into our old friend Captain Qados? Maybe give him a little hint that we know what he's up to?"

Captain Fedr smiled. A real smile this time. "That would be wonderful. May we listen in?"

Janeway laughed. This Xorm captain had a good attitude. "I don't see why not. Stay tuned."

"Thank you, Captain," he said, and cut the connection.

"Ensign, can you make sure they get this coming discussion without making it seem too obvious?"

"Not a problem, Captain," Kim said.

"Fine," she said, turning to face the image of the swirling neutron star binary. "Hail the *Invincible.*"

She dropped down into her chair and made herself appear completely relaxed.

After a moment Kim said, "On screen."

Captain Qados's reptilian face filled the screen. He was standing, probably trying to use his body to block out anything behind him.

"Yes, Captain," he said.

Janeway saw more of the Qavok's yellowed, broken teeth than she ever wanted to see.

"Just wanted to let you know," Janeway said,

smiling, keeping her posture relaxed, "that we are keeping an eye on your Qborne forces."

Captain Qados's mouth opened, again showing the teeth; then he snapped it closed. Clearly she had rattled him.

Janeway sat forward. "Be warned that any attack against the Xorm vessel *Gravity* will be considered an attack against this ship."

If a reptile could sneer, that's what Captain Qados did at that moment. "You seem to have a fondness for protecting the weak," he said.

"You seem to have a fondness of picking on those who can't defend themselves," Janeway said, smiling. "But *Voyager* can defend itself, as you've seen."

"We shall see," Captain Qados said.

"Is that a threat?" Janeway asked.

"Take it as you like, Captain," Qados said.

"Maybe I should just blow you out of space now and be done with it." Janeway stood, her hand on her comm panel.

Again Captain Qados's mouth opened, then snapped shut.

Janeway added casually, "I guess I'll have to give that idea some thought. Sure would make it easier on us all." She punched the connection off.

Tom broke into applause, while Harry and Chakotay laughed.

"I'm sure that shook him up," Chakotay said.

"Two hours and fifty minutes remaining," the computer said.

Janeway wanted to slap the computer, she was so frustrated. She glanced at Chakotay.

"Don't look at me," he said, smiling. "You're the one who ordered the countdown."

"Remind me never to do that again."

"Oh, I will," Chakotay said. "You can be sure of that."

CHAPTER
15

LIEUTENANT TYLA WATCHED AS CHIEF ENGINEER B'Elanna Torres briefed her captain. Beyond the two women, the Qavok yacht sat, its lines smooth and rounded against the straight, functional lines of the *Voyager* shuttlebay. Beside the yacht, the shuttle looked more powerful. More forceful. More like it could handle any situation. Tyla knew that her hatred of the Qavok was coloring her observation, but she didn't care. The *Voyager* shuttle was just a better-looking craft as far as she was concerned.

"Linking the shuttle and the yacht together solves a number of problems," Torres said to Janeway, pointing at the screen on the panel in front of her. "We can use the shuttle's shields, the shuttle's engines, and the shuttle's navigation system. In essence, the yacht simply becomes cargo attached to the outside."

"And you can get both warp cores to breach at the same instant?" Janeway asked.

"We probably won't have to," Torres said. "When the tidal forces start tearing apart the containment of one, it will do the same to the other. When one blows, the other will do so almost instantly, just adding to the power of the explosion. But, just in case, we are attaching a timing device to both and to the gravitational wave container."

"So how long until you're ready?" Janeway said, studying the screen in front of her.

Tyla couldn't see exactly what the captain was looking at, since she was standing out of the way. The moment B'Elanna had come back from the meeting with the idea of hooking the two ships together, there had been little for Tyla to do but stay out of the way. She had, somehow, managed to do just that.

"We can have both ships ready in fifteen minutes," B'Elanna said. "If the math works out, which I think it might, and when you give the go, we'll launch the shuttle, then use a tractor beam to pull the yacht out of the bay and attach it. That process will take less than three minutes."

"Five to be safe?" Janeway asked. "We've got to consider the conditions outside at the moment."

"Five," B'Elanna nodded.

"Good work," Janeway said to B'Elanna. Then she looked at Tyla. "Both of you."

"Thank you, Captain," Tyla said.

B'Elanna nodded, undoubtedly already thinking about the next problem. Over the last hour or so, Tyla had come to recognize that look.

"I'll check back in thirty minutes," Janeway said, and headed out of the landing bay.

"What do you want me to do next?" Tyla asked B'Elanna, breaking the woman's concentration.

"Actually," B'Elanna said, "the most important thing we've got left to do. I want you to download every ounce of information that's in that yacht's computers, no matter how deep it's buried."

Tyla could feel the excitement twist her stomach. She'd already had the chance to study a Qavok warship in close detail. Now she was going to get the chance to pore through the Qavok prince's computer. Her knowledge was going to be invaluable to the war effort when she got home.

"Gladly," Tyla said.

"Good," B'Elanna said. "You've got less than thirty minutes. Don't waste it."

"I won't," Tyla said. She turned and walked in running steps; she was then inside the swank interior of the yacht and back in the pilot's chair. But this time the feeling of being trapped didn't bother her.

This time she was getting what she wanted.

Janeway found Dr. Maalot and Seven in the lab. One screen to their left showed the containment as it pulled in more and more energy from the neutron star binary. It seemed clear that the experiment had worked wonderfully. Too bad it wasn't the only thing they had to think about at the moment.

Seven stood over a different panel, her fingers flying over the controls. Dr. Maalot stood slightly to one side, a frown on his face, clearly concentrating, working to keep up with Seven.

Janeway didn't want to interrupt an important calculation, so she paused, staying silent until Seven stopped and Dr. Maalot nodded.

"Have you calculated the results of the joined warp-core explosion?" Janeway asked, moving up to stand beside Seven.

"We have, Captain," Seven said. "Ensign Kim was correct. Simultaneous warp-core breaches, plus a set amount of gravitational energy stored in a containment unit on board the shuttle, would generate enough energy to suffice."

"Good," Janeway said. For the first time since all this started, her stomach unclamped a little. "Have you double-checked your calculations?"

"We are doing that now, Captain," Dr. Maalot said. "But I must say, I think this will work."

"It needs to," Janeway said.

"It's ironic," he said, smiling. "A short time ago I was excited just to *see* this neutron star binary. Now I'm working to control it. This is a like a dream come true."

Janeway smiled at the Lekk physicist, then patted him on the shoulder. "Just make sure those calculations are right. We don't want this dream turning into a nightmare."

"I understand, Captain," he said. But the smile didn't dim from his face.

"Seven," Janeway said. "We've also got to double-check the shield calculations. We want to make sure the shuttle and yacht last long enough to get into position."

"I will, Captain," Seven said. "But the flight may require a pilot for all but the last few seconds."

The sentence startled Janeway. She had expected that they would be able to set the autopilot, then beam away at once. "Why?"

"I've calculated the fluctuating gravitational forces coming from the binary. It would not be possible to program an automatic pilot for handling such rapidly changing forces with accuracy."

"Remote control?" Janeway asked. "We could fly the shuttle from *Voyager.*"

"Possible," Seven said. "If you are willing to accept the added elements of risk. This explosion, set off at the wrong time or position, could alter the neutron star's path into a more densely populated area of the galaxy."

Janeway nodded. She understood exactly what Seven was saying. If they were going to do this, they had to make sure it was done correctly. And the best choice for that was a pilot to fly it most of the way in, then beam out. Assuming, of course, that the transporter would work through all the gravitational forces at work. And if it didn't work, it would be far, far too late to stop.

"Understood," Janeway said. "Get the calculations done as quickly as possible. The shuttles should be standing by within a half-hour."

Seven nodded and turned back to her board.

Dr. Maalot smiled at Janeway. "We won't be long."

"Good," Janeway said.

She didn't say, "Just be right."

"One hour and fifty minutes remaining," the computer said.

Janeway shifted in her command chair and stared at the swirling binary neutron star on the screen. She thought about shutting the countdown off, but decided she would let it run twice more. After that, there would no longer be a point.

Beside her Chakotay said, "I won't be sorry to hear the last of that thing."

"I'll second that," Tom said.

Janeway smiled. Tom's uniform was stained with sweat. He hadn't moved from his pilot's chair for hours. His hands were constantly in motion as he worked to keep the orbit of *Voyager* stable against the incredible forces at work around them. Only twice in the last two hours had the ship even shuddered slightly. And Tom had sworn both times.

They were lucky to have a pilot of Tom's ability. He'd saved the ship more than once over the last few years. If she had to pick a pilot to fly that shuttle down into that binary, it wouldn't be him. Taking Tom away from the main pilot's chair would threaten all the lives on *Voyager* and she wasn't willing to do that.

But then who would pilot the shuttle?

She glanced at her second-in-command and best friend. Chakotay was the second-best shuttle pilot they had. Tuvok was the third. It would have to be one of them.

She stood and looked at her security officer. "Mr. Tuvok, has the situation with the Qavok changed?"

"No, Captain," he said.

"Okay, I need to talk to you in my ready room." She glanced at Chakotay. "Commander, would you join us?"

"Gladly," Chakotay said.

It took her only a few minutes to completely relay the conversation with Seven to her two officers. Then she finished with "I will not send Tom and risk all the lives on *Voyager*. We need him where he is."

"Agreed," Chakotay said. "I'll take the shuttle down."

"It would be logical that I fly the shuttle, Commander," Tuvok said.

Janeway laughed. She knew, without a doubt,

that both her officers would have that exact reaction when faced with this problem.

"Explain the logic, Tuvok," Janeway said.

"You are needed for your scientific abilities in this type of situation, Captain. When you are pulled from command for such matters, you must have an experienced officer in command on the bridge. As security officer, I am the most easily replaced in this instance. Since I am also rated as the third-best shuttle pilot, I am the logical choice."

She glanced at Chakotay. "Hard to argue with such reason, isn't it?"

Chakotay smiled. "Yeah. Annoying, also."

Tuvok glanced at the commander. "I did not intend to be annoying. I was simply answering the captain's question."

Janeway and Chakotay both laughed.

"You were fine," Janeway said. "But before we send you out to risk your life on this flight, I need you to test the transporter system closer to the binary."

"Logical," Tuvok said. "We can send off a probe and lock on to it with the transporter to run tests."

"Good," Janeway said. "Get to it and report as soon as you can."

Tuvok turned and moved back onto the bridge. After he had left, Janeway smiled at Chakotay. "Sorry. I know you would have wanted to do the flying."

Chakotay laughed softly. "Yeah, but hard to argue with Vulcan logic."

"Why do you suppose," Janeway said, dropping down behind her desk, "that doesn't make me feel any better?"

Chakotay had no answer to that one.

CHAPTER

16

JANEWAY STOOD BESIDE ENSIGN KIM IN THE COMMUNI-cations area of the bridge. Harry was frantically working to adjust the calibration on the transport-er so that it could maintain a lock on the probe in the intense gravitational and radiation forces flow-ing from the spinning binary neutron star.

So far they had lost two probes.

She wasn't happy about that. She wasn't happy about condemning one of her crew to death for some harebrained idea. They would have to find a way to get Tuvok out of that shuttle at the right time.

"Ready," Harry said.

"Do it, Mr. Tuvok," Janeway said.

A moment later Tuvok said, "Probe away."

To Janeway, time seemed to stop on the bridge as she and Harry both watched the board.

It all seemed fine for the first few seconds; then the transporter lock on the probe started to weaken. Exactly as it had done on the first two probes.

Harry's fingers flew over his controls and the lock strengthened again, just in time.

"Ten seconds to correct height," Tuvok said.

The correct height, as Tuvok had said, was just before the point where the tidal forces of the binary would tear the shuttles apart and set off the warp-core breaches.

Two seconds between saving Tuvok's life and losing it.

Two very short seconds.

Again the lock weakened and for an instant Janeway thought Harry had lost it. But it remained as he adjusted, seemingly reading the intense variable forces before they hit the probe.

"Five seconds."

Harry still had a transporter lock on the probe. But he was fighting it. He had managed to stay with this probe far longer than the first two. It seemed the practice was helping.

"Three." Tuvok started the countdown.

Harry still had the lock.

"Two."

Still . . .

"One."

"Beam that probe back," Janeway ordered.

Harry's fingers were now really flying over the

controls as he fought the probe into the transporter buffer.

"Got it!" he said, smiling up at the captain.

"One and a half seconds before the binary would have torn it apart on a molecular level even with its protective screen."

"Good job, Harry," Janeway said. "Drop it in the cargo bay."

"In the bay," Kim said, letting out a sigh.

"Can you download the information out of it?"

"No," Harry said after a moment. "It's too damaged."

Janeway nodded. "I'll go see if I can salvage anything. But in the meantime, I want you two to repeat this exercise. Do it over and over if you have to. I want to make sure we can do the same thing every time. Understood?"

"Yes, Captain," Tuvok said. "Prepare, Ensign."

"Give me thirty seconds," Harry said. "I want to make one more adjustment."

Harry went back to work as Janeway headed for the door. That probe would tell them exactly what kind of forces to expect—if she could get the information out of it and download it to Seven and Dr. Maalot. It would be very helpful to make sure their calculations were correct.

"One hour and twenty minutes remaining," the computer said.

"I know, I know," Janeway said as she reached the door.

Behind her, on the bridge, she heard both Tom

and Chakotay laugh. She obviously said that a little too loud.

Janeway studied the exterior of the probe. It looked as if it had been put through a meat grinder. But somehow it had remained intact and collecting data. It took her less than five minutes to get the data to Seven. By the time she got there, Seven had incorporated the data into their calculations.

"Does anything change?" Janeway asked as she moved up between Seven and Dr. Maalot.

"Nothing, Captain," Seven said. "Our initial calculations were accurate."

Seven keyed up a schematic of the neutron star binary. Then she set in motion the entire picture, bringing an image of the shuttle in from above. "The shuttle must be at this height, at this exact moment," Seven said, bringing up the height and time on the screen.

"The force of the two warp-core ruptures, plus the gravitational-energy-container rupture, will be focused on this area of the secondary neutron star, which is becoming more bloated as it loses matter.

On the screen Seven brought up a blast point on the surface of the less massive of the two neutron stars.

"Thus causing it to explode exactly two point three nine milliseconds sooner," Dr. Maalot said.

"Do you believe this will work, Seven?" Janeway asked.

Seven stared at the screen for a moment. "Yes, I

do. I must admit that my earlier opinions were in error in a number of factors. For that, Captain, I apologize."

"No need, Seven," Janeway said. "We're all learning from this one time."

"I do not foresee another time," Seven said.

"Nor do I," Janeway said. "Thank heavens."

She tapped her comm badge. "B'Elanna, are the shuttles ready?"

"They are, Captain," B'Elanna said. "But I think you might want to take a look at what Tyla found."

"On my way," Janeway said.

Tyla managed to contain her dread at showing the captain what she had found. She didn't know these humans very well, yet. And she had no idea how a powerful human captain like Janeway would react to news.

Janeway strode into the hangar bay, looking intent and worried. Tyla could clearly tell the woman was carrying a heavy burden. She was making decisions that would affect entire systems full of beings.

"What do you have?" Janeway asked as she approached Tyla.

"I was downloading the information from the yacht's computer," Tyla said, "to make sure we didn't miss anything that would be useful to us against the Qavok."

"Good idea," Janeway said.

"B'Elanna thought of it," Tyla said.

Janeway nodded to B'Elanna.

"I discovered a link," Tyla said. "Buried under passwords and command codes."

"To what?" Janeway asked.

"At first I didn't know," Tyla said. "I just knew it was a link of some sort. But once I got past the security features, I discovered there was a secondary computer aboard."

"Really?" Janeway said softly, her eyebrows raising above her closely set eyes. "What was the reason for that?"

"It seems," Tyla said, "that the computer was used as a command storage area. All Qavok military plans and operations were automatically downloaded to the second computer and stored. If the prince was using the yacht, he could then always be in touch with whatever operation was going on in the Qavok Empire."

"No wonder they were so angry when you took it," Janeway said, smiling at Tyla.

"Yes," Tyla said, feeling a little more relaxed now. "It does make sense."

"And we've downloaded all this information from both computers?" Janeway asked.

"We have," B'Elanna said. "But Tyla found this in the process."

B'Elanna keyed in a screen and a report appeared, filled with pictures of a round ship of some sort.

"What is it?" Janeway asked, scanning the page as quickly as she could.

"We think it's what the Qavok plan to use to change the course of the neutron star," Tyla said before B'Elanna could answer. She wanted to make sure that if anyone was punished for delivering the bad news, it would be her. She found it, she took responsibility for it.

"What?" Janeway said.

"Sure looks like it, Captain," B'Elanna said. "Extra-strong forward shields, no real passenger room, no real bridge area, very large warp core. And no weapons."

"And it seems to have been built for one flight," Tyla said. "Qavok only build ships with weapons, so that they can fight. They would never build a ship without a weapon, unless it was to be used to trigger another weapon."

"The neutron star binary," Janeway said.

"The binary," Tyla said, agreeing. "To attack my homeworld."

"Well," Janeway said, "that isn't going to happen. Especially now that you've found this. Good work."

Tyla nodded, not letting her relief show. "Thank you."

"You two make sure every detail of the shuttle and yacht is ready. And transfer the gravitational container to the shuttle when Seven tells you it's time."

"We'll be ready," B'Elanna said.

Tyla watched as the captain left the shuttlebay, walking as quickly as she had come in. "She's an amazing captain," Tyla said, more to herself than to B'Elanna.

"Captain Janeway?" B'Elanna asked, glancing up. Then she nodded. "You are right about that. Now get back to work. I want you scanning that information from the secondary computer. See if you can find anything more we might use."

"Gladly," Tyla said. Digging in the most top-secret files of her enemy made her feel like a child in a room full of candy. There was so much good stuff, she just didn't know where to start.

She just hoped that Captain Janeway would give the files to her when this was all over.

CHAPTER

17

"FIFTY MINUTES REMAINING," THE COMPUTER SAID.

"All right, that's it. Turn off that stupid reminder," Janeway said. She was standing beside Ensign Kim, going over the data from the last three successful retrievals of probes.

"Gladly, Captain," Chakotay said.

"Thank you," she said, ignoring his smile.

She went back to studying the probe retrieval reports. Ensign Kim had gotten better and better at holding a lock on the probe and then transporting it back at the exact right moment.

"Tuvok," Janeway said, glancing up at her security officer. "You feel comfortable enough to risk your life on this?"

"I do, Captain," Tuvok said. "The risk is minor compared with the reward of success."

Janeway nodded. "I'm glad you feel that way. Ensign Kim, you think you can get him out of there at the right time?"

"I do, Captain," Kim said.

"Good. Tuvok, get to the shuttlebay and make sure you're familiar with how B'Elanna has the shuttle and yacht connection worked out. Then stand by there for launch."

"Understood," Tuvok said. He started for the door.

"And good luck," Janeway said, smiling at her friend.

"I would rather depend on skill and percentages," he said. "But thank you."

He stepped through the door and she moved down to her chair. "Harry, keep an eye on those long-range scans. If the Qavok are going to move, they'll be doing it soon. They've got to set off their explosion ahead of ours."

"Yes, Captain," Kim said.

"How are you doing, Tom?" she asked. His shirt was soaked in sweat and his hair was damp. He never took his eyes away from his control panel.

"It's getting rougher by the hour," he said. "But I'll last until we're away from here."

"Good," she said. "Can I have Mr. Neelix bring you anything?"

"Doing fine," he said. "Thanks."

She dropped down into her chair and let herself, for the first time in the last hour, study the binary on the screen. Even visually, it was clear the end was near. The two stars almost looked as if they had a ring around them as matter was ripped off and flung away from the distended secondary.

"Everything ready?" Chakotay asked.

Janeway glanced over at her second-in-command. He'd been stuck on the bridge while she, Seven, B'Elanna, and the two Lekk guests had been getting everything ready. "All set," she said. "Seven and Dr. Maalot have gone over the math more times than I care to think about."

Chakotay laughed. "And they both loved it, I'll bet."

"Can't speak for Seven," Janeway said, "but you're right on the money with Dr. Maalot.

"Lieutenant Tyla also found a second computer on board the yacht, loaded with Qavok military plans and information."

"Gold mine for her," Chakotay said. "You going to let her keep the information after all this is over?"

"I don't honestly know yet," Janeway said. "I'm not sure how far past the Prime Directive we are here, trying to save these planets in the first place. And I'm not sure how much further I want to go in this situation."

"She did capture the yacht herself," Chakotay said. "And she was the one who found them."

"Always loopholes," Janeway said, smiling.

The ship bumped hard and Janeway grabbed for her chair to hold herself in position.

Another sharp bump, and then the deck seemed to shudder and settle back to its normal, calm state.

"Sorry, Captain," Tom said as his fingers flew over his controls. "Getting worse and worse out there."

"You're doing fine, Captain Proton," Janeway said.

Tom glanced around at her and smiled. Then he turned back to his work.

"What's left to do?" Chakotay asked.

Janeway stared at the binary, then said, "Nothing but wait. We're actually ready early."

"Seems the countdown helped," Chakotay said.

"Surprised to hear that from you." Janeway grinned. "I thought you found it irritating."

"Let's just say it grew on me," Chakotay said. "In any case, we are ready."

"Yeah," Janeway said, softly, never taking her gaze from the screen. "We sure are."

She just wished she felt as certain as she sounded.

Seven unhooked the energy containment from its connection with the outside filters and sealed the container. The standing waves of gravitational force were bouncing from the sides of the container in such a way as to keep any feedback problems from building up in it. It was a shame that such an incredible store of energy had to be used in this fashion. Seven doubted they would ever again have the chance to gather this much, or solve the problems of how to use it.

She placed the container inside a security force-field to make sure it remained stable, then lifted the entire thing with an antigrav carrying unit. "Step ahead of me," she told Dr. Maalot. "We must deliver this to the shuttlebay."

Dr. Maalot strode out ahead of Seven enthusiastically while she focused on moving the container smoothly and slowly to its final destination. She supposed it was lucky that this experiment in gravitational wave energy containment had worked. Otherwise, the two warp-core breaches of the small ships would not have been enough to get the desired results. It was only the release of this energy at the same moment that even allowed this plan a chance of success.

Dr. Maalot had the shuttlebay door open and Seven floated the containment through.

"In the shuttle," Torres said, moving to open the door for Seven.

"This must remain mounted inside the security forcefield," Seven said. "That way it will ride safely until the moment it is needed."

"I got that," B'Elanna said. "Don't worry."

"I am not worrying," Seven said, wondering, not for the first time, why her crewmates were constantly projecting their own pesky emotions onto her. "I am simply stating an instruction."

Lieutenant Tuvok turned as Seven entered and studied what she and B'Elanna were doing. Beside Tuvok stood Lieutenant Tyla. She too was just watching.

As Seven held the containment steady, Torres secured it to the inside of the shuttle. After a minute the engineer said, "Remove the antigrav unit now."

Seven did as she was told and stepped back. The containment held as B'Elanna ran a series of checks on it.

"Done," B'Elanna said, smiling after the last scan. "I can think of a hundred better uses for this energy."

"Assuming that we could control its release," Seven said.

"Yeah," B'Elanna said. "Assuming."

"We will never know if we would have succeeded now," Seven said.

"You have succeeded in containing the energy," Tuvok said. "Such success does not preclude success in the future."

"It is an amazing feat," Dr. Maalot said, his voice broadcasting admiration. "A fantastic accomplishment."

"Agreed," Tuvok said.

Torres only snorted.

"Thank you," Seven said. Deep inside she could feel a small part of her taking in the compliments and being proud of the accomplishment. She did not dwell on the feeling. Simply noted it. She would think to ask Captain Janeway about such feeling later, if the opportunity presented itself. It might make for an interesting discussion.

"Captain," Ensign Kim said. "I'm picking up three Qavok ships on long-range scan. Heading this way."

Janeway snapped around. Thirty-one minutes until the Qavok had to explode their device to change the path of the neutron star into the Lekk system. They might be ornery, but they were also punctual.

"Can you get a reading on the ships?" Chakotay asked, standing and moving up to Tuvok's position.

Kim frowned for a moment, then said, "Two Qavok warships and a ship of unknown design between them."

"Round in shape?" Janeway asked.

"Yes," Kim said.

"The ship Lieutenant Tyla found the plans for. Good. At least we know what we're up against."

"That will help," Chakotay said.

"Captain," Kim said. "The other eleven Qavok warships are slowly leaving position to join the three new ships."

"Estimated time of arrival?"

"Twenty-eight minutes," Kim said.

"Captain," Tom said. "We'll be a sitting duck if we stay in this low orbit for a fight."

"Understood," Janeway said.

"Captain," Kim said. "The thirty troops on the *Invincible* have locked down in two shuttles. They appear to be getting ready to launch."

She shook her head in amazement and turned back to stare at the binary filling the screen. Thirteen Qavok warships on the way. Another already in orbit. All arrayed against *Voyager* and a Xorm science ship. If Tuvok were here, he would most certainly tell her how slim the odds were of survival. But at the moment, he was facing his own slim odds.

"Ensign," Janeway said. "Hail the *Gravity*."

"On screen," Kim said a few moments later.

"We've seen the Qavok movement," Captain Fedr said. "This doesn't look good."

"No it doesn't," Janeway said. "The round ship is one they built specially to dive into the neutron star binary. Nothing but screens and a large warp core."

Captain Fedr shook his head slowly from side to side, clearly amazed. "You know, I sometimes don't give the Qavok enough credit for pure evil."

"By trying to destroy an entire inhabited system," Janeway said, "I'd say that *pure evil* just about describes them."

"So what are we going to do to stop them?" Fedr asked.

"I think," Janeway said, "that it might be a wise idea if you pulled off to a safe distance and stayed out of the fight. Let us handle them."

"Thirteen Qavok warships?" Captain Fedr said,

almost laughing. "Captain, I know your ship is powerful, but there are limits to everything. It would help if I drew a few of those warships' attention. Even the odds a little. And don't worry. We can take care of ourselves just fine."

"Thank you, Captain," Janeway said. "Your help is gladly accepted."

"No, the thanks belong to you," Captain Fedr said. "It's just lucky for all of us you came along when you did."

"Let's see how this turns out first," Janeway said, smiling at the Xorm. "Follow my lead and move up to a higher orbit where we have more room to fight."

"Actually, Captain," Fedr said, "I'm thinking I should take my ship slightly lower."

"Lower?"

"Exactly," Captain Fedr said. "I have a skilled pilot and a ship designed to withstand battering. We'll set up to block the path of their special ship. If a few of those warships come down to clear us out of the way, we'll have the advantage."

"Good thinking," Janeway said.

"Thank you," Fedr said.

"One more thing," Janeway said. "The Qborne troops are about to launch from the *Invincible* in two shuttles. Any idea what we should do about them?"

"One moment," Fedr said.

He did a slight bit of work below him, off screen;

then beside his face an illustration of a Qavok warship appeared.

"Captain," he said, "the Qavok shuttlebay doors are here."

On the illustration a red circle appeared around an area of the Qavok ship. Of course, Janeway knew that, but said nothing, letting the Xorm captain go on with his idea.

"A preemptive strike against the *Invincible,*" he said, "hitting this area, would lock those shuttlebay doors closed, and render the Qborne irrelevant. If they can't get out, they can't hurt anything."

"Got it," Janeway said, turning back to Captain Fedr. "And good luck to you in the upcoming fight. We'll stop them."

"I certainly hope so, Captain," Fedr said. "May the gods be with you over the next hour."

Janeway broke the connection. "Hail Captain Qados."

"On screen," Kim said.

The sneering, reptilian face of the Qavok appeared. Now, after getting a pretty solid confirmation that they were purposely trying to destroy an entire system, she was so angry she could barely talk.

"Captain Qados," Janeway said before the Qavok could even say a word. "We know you are planning an attack against the Xorm ship with a group of Qborne. Either have them unload from your shuttles or face the consequences."

Janeway cut the connection before the Qavok could even say a word.

"Fair warning," Chakotay said. "Very restrained. How long do we wait?"

"We move the moment those shuttlebay doors start to open. Seal them solid. Then target the *Invincible*'s weapons and engines and take them out. Might as well drop the odds a little right off the bat."

"Targeted and standing by," Chakotay said.

"All right, people," Janeway said, settling into her chair. "Take us to red alert. Tom, move us up out of this orbit."

"Gladly," Tom said.

Around her the lights changed to a red tint and the computer announced red alert, battle stations to the crew.

On the screen in front of her the binary neutron star continued to tear itself apart.

What a stupid place to fight a battle was all she could think. *Really, really stupid.*

CHAPTER
18

DR. MAALOT WATCHED IN SHOCK AS THE LIGHTS around the shuttlebay dimmed and turned red. "Battle stations," the voice came over the comm system. "All crew to battle stations."

Suddenly the large bay transformed from an inviting workplace to a cavern of urgency and doom. On the walls red lights blinked, and the air seemed suddenly heavy.

At a run, and without a word, both B'Elanna and Seven left the shuttlebay. Both, it seemed, were heading for Engineering, or maybe the bridge. Dr. Maalot didn't know.

He moved over to where Tyla stood beside the Qavok yacht. She looked calm and collected. He supposed she was used to this type of thing. But for the life of him he couldn't imagine how anyone could get used to fighting. It just wasn't something he understood.

"Any idea what we're supposed to do?"

"None," she said, shrugging. She clicked off the display of Qavok military files in front of her and turned to face him. "Stay out of the way, I would guess."

"I'd much rather help, if I could," Maalot said. And he honestly would, for two reasons. First, he felt he owed these humans a great deal, not only for saving his life, but for what they were trying to do to stop the Qavok. And second, he hated what the Qavok were thinking of doing to his homeworld. They simply had to be stopped.

"So would I," Lieutenant Tyla said. "I'd love to get my hands around the neck of a Qavok and just squeeze."

"That is not exactly the type of help I was thinking of," he said. He could tell that she meant what she said. He looked around. There had to be something they could do.

"We should check in with Lieutenant Tuvok in the shuttle," Tyla said, moving in that direction.

"True," Maalot said. "Excellent idea. He very well might have something for us to do. Or at least we can find out what is happening outside this bay."

Tyla led the way and he tried to stay at her side, but failed miserably. Her stride was just longer than his.

Each time he had stepped inside the shuttle, he had been struck by not only the simple elegance of it, but the efficiency. The prince's yacht was, by contrast, an oversized decadent toy.

Maalot moved in and stood by a rear chair above a communication and environmental-control panel. Tyla instantly moved up and sat in the copilot's chair next to Lieutenant Tuvok. It seemed like a natural position for her. It was a chair he would never have thought of sitting in unless someone forced him to.

"We're looking for something to do to help," Maalot said.

Tyla nodded as Tuvok glanced up at her, then around at Maalot.

"There is little that needs to be done at the moment," Tuvok said.

"Could you at least tell us what is happening?"

Tuvok worked over the control panel for a moment, then turned. "Thirteen Qavok warships are on an intercept course for this location. They are escorting the round ship of which you discovered the plans. There is also a warship in orbit attempting to launch an assault against the Xorm science ship for a reason not easily determined."

"The round ship?" Tyla asked. "Is that the ship they want to fly into the neutron star?"

"That would be the logical assumption of use for such a ship," Tuvok said, again working over his controls.

"Thirteen warships on the way," Dr. Maalot said.

"Another in orbit. How can *Voyager* fight that many off?"

There was no way he could see the humans winning this fight. They were doomed. The thought made him shudder.

"Captain," Kim said, *"Invincible's* shuttlebay doors are starting to open."

"Stop them," Janeway ordered.

Voyager had moved to a slightly higher orbit, but was pacing *Invincible* and was still well within phaser range of the Qavok warship. Also the Xorm ship *Gravity* had moved farther down. It now somehow orbited just above the orbit where Ensign Kim had transported out the probes. How the Xorm ship was managing to maintain that orbit was beyond her. But for the moment it was.

Voyager rocked slightly as the phaser beams shot out.

The Qavok warship's screens flared for almost two seconds and then went down. The phaser beams then hit the area where the shuttlebay doors were, exploding the area and sealing the doors shut in the ruins. Janeway knew, without a doubt, that they were lucky their weapons and shields were a factor more powerful than the Qavok's. Otherwise, they would have been dead before now.

"Direct hit," Chakotay said. "Those shuttles will never be launched."

On screen Janeway could see the red, melting metal on the side of the Qavok warship. Then there was a small explosion inside that area of the ship, sending material spinning out into space. No doubt one of the shuttles had had a small accident.

At that moment the *Invincible* fired back, lighting up *Voyager*'s screens in various shades of pink and red. The impact rocked the bridge slightly, but not enough to make her even grab her chair for support.

"No damage," Kim said. "Shields holding at ninety-nine percent. Now back to one hundred percent."

"Hit them again, Ensign," Janeway said. "And make sure they can't go anywhere real soon."

Again *Voyager*'s phasers shot out, picking at the *Invincible* as if cutting a moldy spot out of a block of cheese.

"Weapons destroyed," Chakotay said. "Fires and explosions in the shuttlebay and in the weapons areas. Both their ion drive and warp capabilities are off-line. They do have enough maneuvering thrusters to remain in their current orbit for some time, however."

Janeway nodded. "Good, we'll let them go at that. As long as they don't get in our way."

"Twelve minutes until the main fleet arrives," Kim said.

"Switch the screen to them," Janeway said.

The image of the thirteen warships flying in a rough formation filled the screen. In their center was the round sphere of a ship, clearly being protected by the warships. She had no idea how they were going to fight thirteen warships. Granted, *Voyager*'s shields and weapons were far superior to the Qavok's, but not when multiplied synergetically thirteen times. Even five or six ships attacking at once might prove to be too much firepower for *Voyager* to handle.

"I'm open to ideas now," Janeway said.

Silence filled the bridge as the red lights blinked softly in the background.

"Okay," Janeway said after a very long moment of silence that made the bridge feel more like the inside of a tomb than a starship control center. "Let's narrow this problem down some. We know we can easily handle three or four of the Qavok at the same time. So how do we get their numbers down to that, yet not allow them to get that round ship through to the binary?"

Again silence. Then Ensign Kim said hesitantly, "Captain, how about the shuttle?"

"Of course," she said. "Good work, Ensign."

The shuttle's screens and weapons were powerful enough to hold off at least two or three of the Qavok warships without a problem. And if Tuvok could work it right, he might just get a shot at that center ship while *Voyager* drew most of their fire. Then, if they survived and stopped the Qavok, they would have eight or so minutes to launch the yacht, get both hooked together, and get them into position. It would be cutting the timing extremely close, but it just might work.

"Janeway to shuttle. Tuvok?"

"Go ahead, Captain."

"I think we're going to need your help in this fight."

"Yes, Captain," he said.

"I'll send a copilot to help you, so hang on."

"There is no need," Tuvok said. "Lieutenant Tyla is beside me and would serve satisfactorily in that position. Dr. Maalot is at the communications panel."

"Dr. Maalot? Lieutenant Tyla, would you like to help us on this?"

"Gladly," Dr. Maalot said. His voice was thin and almost cracked, but it was clear he wanted to help.

"It would be an honor to copilot this craft with Mr. Tuvok," Lieutenant Tyla said.

"Thank you," Janeway said. "Launch when ready. After the fight let's hope we have time for you to come back for the yacht."

"Captain," Chakotay said. "The energy containment?"

Janeway felt her stomach clamp up even tighter than it had been a few moments before. Chakotay was right. There was no way the shuttle could go into battle with that much energy riding inside it.

"Torres to shuttlebay," Janeway said into the ship's comm line. "Emergency."

"On my way," B'Elanna's voice came back strong.

"Tuvok," Janeway said. "Hold on. We've got to get that energy containment out of there."

"Dr. Maalot is already working on preparing it for a move," Tuvok said.

Janeway glanced at Chakotay with a relieved look.

"How much time do we have, Ensign?" Janeway asked.

"Eight minutes," Kim said.

"We could start another countdown," Tom said.

"Just drive, mister," Janeway said.

Tom had his back to her, but she could tell he was smiling.

B'Elanna almost ran into the shuttlebay interior doors as they opened too slowly for her fast dash. Inside the bay, the shuttle's doors were open and she could see both Dr. Maalot and Tuvok working over the energy containment canister. There was no chance of a rupture. No chance at all. She was convinced that the container design was safe. Or at least as safe as anything that held that much bottled-up energy.

She ducked inside the shuttle. "What's wrong?"

"We are using the shuttle in the coming battle," Tuvok said. "We must move this to the yacht before I can launch."

"Good idea," she said. "Might have proved fatal otherwise."

"It's almost ready to be moved," Dr. Maalot said.

"Stand back," B'Elanna said.

Dr. Maalot instantly moved aside and B'Elanna quickly checked all the readings.

Stable and fine.

Energy holding constant inside.

Good. Very good.

She grabbed the antigravity unit and quickly attached it, then floated the canister up as Tuvok released it from the wall of the shuttle. She felt as though she were walking with a live torpedo through the halls. One bump would set it off. Of course, it was nowhere near that unstable. Nope, not unstable at all.

Moving slowly and carefully, she got the canister out into the open area of the shuttlebay deck.

"Safe to launch," she said over her shoulder to Tuvok.

Tuvok nodded and the shuttle's hatch slid closed without him saying another word.

"Well, good-bye to you, too," she said to no one in particular.

"How are you doing, B'Elanna?" Janeway's voice asked, filling the shuttlebay.

"Got the energy containment out of the shuttle and it's launching. I'll secure it in the yacht."

"Very good," Janeway said, and cut the connection.

B'Elanna moved back against the wall as the shuttle moved toward the opening bay doors and the forcefield that kept the atmosphere inside.

Then the shuttle was through the field and out into space, and the big doors were closing.

"Okay," B'Elanna said to the energy containment canister. "Let's get you secure in the yacht and get back to work."

One minute before the battle broke out, the container was locked against a wall inside the yacht's engine room and B'Elanna was sprinting for Engineering. She had a sneaking hunch that with the odds that faced them, she was going to be needed very quickly.

CHAPTER
19

"SHUTTLE LAUNCHED," ENSIGN KIM SAID.

On the main screen in front of her, Janeway faced the imposing spectacle of thirteen Qavok warships, all coming in hard and staying together around the center ship. They looked like a flock of birds in flight. A flock of very ugly and dangerous birds.

She took a slow, deep breath and tried to relax her tight shoulders. These ships were Qavok ships, not Klingon or Cardassian. These ships, one-on-one, were no match for *Voyager* in any area. She knew she should think of them as a bunch of scruffy wild dogs. It was only in numbers that they got really dangerous. As long as she remembered that, they would come out of this just fine.

"How long until they are within range?" she asked.

"Five minutes," Chakotay said. "And eight minutes until they must have their bomb ship in place."

"Bomb ship?" Janeway asked, turning slightly and smiling.

Chakotay was manning Tuvok's station. He shrugged. "Seemed like a logical name for it."

"Fine by me," she said. "Mr. Kim, please put up a location schematic in the upper right quarter of the main screen. I want to track them all if we break them up."

"Understood," Kim said. A moment later a small area schematic appeared. In the center of it was the neutron star binary. The Qavok warships were shown with red dots coming on the screen from the left. The bomb ship was black, and the Xorm scientific ship was orange. *Voyager* and the shuttle were both green dots.

"Ensign, open a channel between *Voyager* and the shuttle and keep it open."

"Open, Captain."

"Mr. Tuvok," Janeway said.

"One moment, Captain," Dr. Maalot's voice said.

Janeway smiled.

"Yes, Captain," Tuvok said.

"I'm going to take *Voyager* and move right. You go left. The instant you are within range, open fire.

We're going to need every bit of help we can get on this one."

"Understood, Captain," Tuvok said. "Lieutenant Tyla has reported that in her research of the Qavok military, she has discovered that the weakest area of their shields is aft and lower."

"Aft and lower," Janeway said, glancing back at Chakotay, who nodded. "Got it."

"That area," Tuvok said, "is above their engine rooms and drive area. A single shot should, if placed correctly, immobilize the entire ship."

"Very good," Janeway said. "Tell Lieutenant Tyla thanks. Chakotay, change of plans. You stay in this position. We'll take *Voyager* over and behind them and attack from there."

"Yes, Captain," Chakotay said.

"Tom," Janeway said, "lay in a course that will flash us over and come in behind those ships at phaser range. Warp six."

"Warp six?" Tom said. "Got it. You want to get past them without a shot being fired."

"Exactly," Janeway said. "Can you do it?"

"Of course."

"Then do it quickly."

Tom nodded and went to work.

"Commander," Janeway said, "set the computer to lay down automatic fire at those aft shields the moment we drop out of warp."

"Got it," he said.

"Course laid in, Captain," Tom said.

"Ready, Commander?"

"Ready," Chakotay said.

"Do it, Tom."

Voyager turned slightly and then jumped to warp, moving above the fleet of ships before the enemy had time to realize what was happening. Then Tom swung wide and brought them in from behind.

"Dropping out of warp in ten seconds," he said.

"Phasers ready," Chakotay said.

Janeway sat and watched as the entire thing seemed to unfold in slow motion.

Thirteen enemy ships, all in formation, had just passed them, moving toward the neutron star binary. On the schematic it first appeared as if *Voyager* were running away. Then slowly the green dot turned and moved in behind the multiple dots of the Qavok fleet.

"Three," Tom said. "Two. One. Now. Dropping out of warp."

Instantly *Voyager*'s phasers fired.

One shot right after another.

But the Qavok screens were holding. With each short blast of a *Voyager* phaser a Qavok warship's rear shields flared to red and then beyond, but just barely held.

The last time that would have cut through those screens and the ships like a hot knife through butter.

"They've managed to strengthen all their shields somehow," Kim said. "I don't know how but I'm reporting at least fifty percent stronger than our first encounter."

"Longer phaser blasts!" Janeway ordered. "Chakotay, go to a full two seconds."

Chakotay nodded, never looking up from his board, and instantly the phaser shots again rocked *Voyager* as they fired. This time the shields on the warships dropped, but the phaser shot didn't last long enough to do enough damage on their surfaces.

"Going to three seconds," Chakotay shouted.

"Tuvok," Janeway said. "Three-second phaser blasts at least."

"Understood," his voice came back.

Six of the Qavok warships had turned and formed a group facing *Voyager*. Seven remained with the bomb ship bearing down on Tuvok and the shuttle.

Four Qavok ships fired at once.

Voyager rocked backward.

"Shields holding," Kim said. "Ninety percent."

Janeway nodded. At least the strength of their weapons hadn't changed.

"Firing," Chakotay said.

Two of the Qavok ships' shields flared to red and then went down. A few moments later both ships exploded.

"Two down," Tom said, "eleven to go."

The other four facing *Voyager* fired again.

Direct hits on the forward screens. Janeway held on as *Voyager* tried to buck her out of her chair.

Again Chakotay fired.

Two more Qavok warships' shields flared and went down. And then a moment later two more ships exploded.

"Screens down to sixty percent," Kim said, "and we have reports of damage coming from all over the ship."

The remaining two warships broke off and rejoined the main group, now cut down to nine.

"How long until that fleet gets into the shuttle's firing range?" Janeway asked.

"Two minutes, thirty seconds," Kim said.

"Mr. Paris," Janeway said. "Can you get us back near the shuttle in time?"

"I can do my best," he said.

"Do it," Janeway said. "Engage when ready. Ensign, tell Mr. Tuvok we are on the way and to stand firm."

She sat back and stared at the schematic. This was not going well so far.

Not at all.

Their first attempt had failed. They had needed to cut that fleet in half for them to stand any chance at all. And now that the Qavok had managed to fortify their shields since the first battle, that was going to be even harder. This ship, let alone the shuttle, would never withstand a direct hit from six or seven of those warships at once.

Tom worked quickly at his station.

Around her the seconds seemed to tick past. The

silence on the bridge was the loudest she had heard in a long time.

Suddenly the ship jumped into warp, heading back right at the neutron star binary, as if it were diving into the death that awaited there.

Maybe it was.

But they had to at least try to stop that bomb ship.

And then, if they were lucky, change the course of the star.

Lieutenant Tyla watched as the fleet of Qavok warships bore down on her and the small *Voyager* shuttle. Tuvok had her manning the phasers and she knew exactly what she needed to do. But still her hands shook slightly. This was the first time she ever remembered that happening in a battle.

But this was also the first time she was facing down nine Qavok warships in a small shuttle.

She had watched *Voyager's* failure to cut the fleet down significantly with a sinking, almost guilty feeling. She should have predicted that the Qavok would adapt their screens and warned the Xorm captain of that possibility. The way the Qavok warship systems worked, they must have taken energy from every other function on their ships to get that kind of shield power. She had no doubt that they had even cut down on life-support functions for this battle. The Qavok would do something like that.

"Lieutenant?" Tuvok said. "Are you ready?"

"I am," Tyla said.

"One minute, fifteen seconds. Phasers armed and ready?"

"Ready, sir," she said.

"Stand by."

"Lieutenant Tyla," Dr. Maalot said. "Before this starts, I just want to say thank you."

She glanced around at her companion of the last few days. "Why thank me?"

He laughed, although it was clearly a strained laugh. "I got a chance to study a neutron star binary up close, with instruments I could have only dreamed about using before these last few days."

"I'm glad," she said.

"No, you don't understand," he said. "Just in case we don't make it through the next few minutes, I want to thank you for getting me to this point, for rescuing me from the Qavok and for giving me the chance to do what most scientists in the galaxy would give their life to do. It has been worth it."

"You're welcome," she said, smiling at him. "But I have no plans on us dying anytime shortly. Don't you want to stick around for the final explosion?"

"Of course I do," he said, smiling.

"Then hang on and help where you can," she said. "This may get rough. But we'll make it."

She turned back and nodded to Tuvok, who only nodded in return. She just wished she felt as positive about their near future as she had tried to sound to Dr. Maalot.

"Fifteen seconds," Tuvok said.

"*Voyager* coming from the right," she said.

She almost wanted to cheer. She had been afraid they would have to face the ships on their own and die trying to stop them.

"Tuvok," the captain's voice came in strong. "Break off hard left the moment you are within firing range. Try to destroy the two leading ships on that side, then get out of range quickly."

"Yes, Captain," he said.

"Copy that," Tyla said. "Targeting the two ships on the left leading edge. Phasers locked and ready."

"Hold," Tuvok said. "Five more seconds."

To Tyla the time seemed to stop at that moment. Her finger was poised over the firing control, waiting.

"Two."

Waiting.

"One."

Waiting.

"Now," Tuvok said.

She fired the phaser, making the shuttle jump slightly, as if a surge had just flowed through it. The two beams of the shuttle's phasers cut at the shields of the two leading Qavok warships, sending them almost at once into reds and then to black.

The warships' shields flashed one final time and then were down.

"Yes!" she said.

The phaser shots cut into the unprotected hulls of the warships, burning inward.

After a second, the first warship exploded into flying debris, the large pieces tumbling at them.

Then her world exploded.

Tuvok sheared the shuttle hard left, but Tyla knew he was too late. Three warships opened fire simultaneously on the shuttle, smashing it backward like a child's toy shoved across a slick floor.

"Screens failing!" Dr. Maalot yelled as sparks and smoke filled the shuttle cabin.

Tyla was almost knocked from her seat, but somehow she managed to hang on and keep firing.

A second warship exploded and she moved the phaser to attack one of the firing ships, targeting and locking.

"Thrusters off-line," Tuvok said. "I will try to jump to warp."

"Shields down to twenty percent," Maalot said, his voice barely containing his panic.

One of the firing ships exploded under Tyla's fire, but two more warships added their phaser fire to the remaining two, rocking the shuttle even harder.

Sparks flew everywhere as two panels exploded near Dr. Maalot and he was thrown to the floor.

Smoke choked her, but she didn't let up on the phaser. She was going to pound those Qavok with her last dying breath.

"Going to warp," Tuvok said. "Now."

Instantly the warships vanished behind them as

the shuttle jumped to warp to get out from under the fire.

Then almost instantly the shuttle dropped back into real space.

"Warp drive off-line," Tuvok said. "We're without the ability to maneuver."

"We destroyed three warships," Tyla said as she quickly checked the battle scene behind them. "Damaged a fourth."

"It seems," Tuvok said, "that we did what we could."

"We can't get back in the fight?" Tyla almost shouted. "Why not?"

"As I said," Tuvok calmly replied, "our drives are all damaged beyond immediate repair."

"We still have twenty-percent shields," Dr. Maalot said as he picked himself back up and climbed into his chair again. "Barely, I might add."

Tyla scanned the board in front of her. "We also have phasers still on-line. Just nothing to shoot at."

"True," Tuvok said. "Now we must hope that *Voyager* is victorious. Or we may get a chance to defend ourselves one final time. Dr. Maalot, see if you can increase our shield strength. Lieutenant, please stand by in case we are approached."

"Where are you going?"

"I will attempt to fix basic thrusters," he said.

She nodded as Tuvok climbed from his chair.

Suddenly, just as on the yacht, she felt very alone, sitting in the front seat, waiting to be killed like a bug. But this time, she had something to fight back with if any of those ships decided to try to kill her. She'd at least sting them before dying.

On the screen, out of phaser range, *Voyager* was in the fight of its life. And there wasn't a thing that Tyla could do to help.

She could only sit and watch.

And she hated that.

Hated that more than anything.

She was a fighter. Her job was to fight.

Not watch.

CHAPTER
20

JANEWAY HELD ON TO HER COMMAND CHAIR AS THE ship rocked. For a moment the lights dimmed, then the power came back up. In front of them on the screen it was clear they had taken out two more of the Qavok ships, but somehow, some way, the Qavok had strengthened their shields. She didn't know how that was possible, but it had happened.

Janeway knew they were in trouble. Deep trouble.

One of the warship's combined blasts had knocked out their phasers and torpedoes. Now *Voyager* was simply a sitting duck. On the main screen the remaining six warships shifted position slightly, moving three up front and leaving three to flank their bomb ship.

"B'Elanna," Janeway said. "I need phasers."

She didn't expect an answer. B'Elanna would be working as fast as she could to find and fix the problem.

It had better be very fast, she thought.

She tried to force herself to sit back and study the entire situation, look for another way to win this.

Tuvok and the shuttle had done its share of damage, hitting the Qavok from the side and managing to destroy three before being knocked aside. Tuvok had managed to jump the shuttle to warp for a short burst, just long enough to get out of range and harm's way.

At least for the moment.

It looked as if the shuttle was now dead in space. They had lost contact but sensors reported that all the passengers were alive. Janeway doubted that that shuttle was going to be flying down into any neutron star binary anytime soon, from the looks of it.

So much for their carefully worked plans on how to change a force of nature. If they could stop the Qavok from changing it, that neutron star was headed exactly where nature had wanted it to go.

Again the entire ship rocked around her.

"Screens down to forty percent," Ensign Kim said.

"B'Elanna?"

"Can't do it, Captain." B'Elanna did not even attempt to conceal her frustration. "Phaser controls have been fused all the way through. We won't have any weapons of any sort for at least three hours. And there's no way to go around the fused areas."

Janeway pounded her fist on the panel.

"Tom," she said, "drop us back into a lower orbit. Buy us a few minutes."

Tom did as he was told just as the ship rocked again.

"Thirty percent," Ensign Kim said. "Two or three more hits like that and we'll lose shields."

"Understood," she said. "Bring all power to the forward shields. Keep those up."

If she didn't do something quickly, this was where their long trip home was going to end.

She studied the schematic on the edge of the big screen. Six warships bearing down on them. Behind *Voyager,* in a lower orbit, was the Xorm ship, waiting for its turn in the box. She had hoped to spare them the fight. But it was starting to seem like she wouldn't be around long enough to stop it from happening.

Also showing on the screen was the warship *Invincible,* still holding orbit, but dead without shields, engines, or weapons. At the moment it was on the far side of the neutron star binary in its orbit.

And then there was the shuttle, floating almost off the schematic, useless.

Voyager rocked again as the lead four warships fired at once. Sparks flew from three panels and smoke filled the ceiling area of the bridge.

Suddenly the answer was there, floating on the

screen in the seemingly lifeless form of the shuttle. They were going to hook the yacht to the shuttle, but that plan was now worthless. So why not use the yacht now, to save their lives?

"B'Elanna," Janeway said. "You've got exactly one minute to launch the yacht into those ships."

"Got it, Captain," B'Elanna said. "Good idea. I'm headed there now. But I'll have to shove the thing out the door with a tractor beam."

"Do what you have to do," Janeway said. "I don't care. Just make sure it drifts right at those Qavok ships."

"Yes, Captain," B'Elanna said.

"Before you start," Janeway said, "set a charge to rupture the warp core thirty seconds after leaving. Understand?"

"Way ahead of you," B'Elanna said, breathlessly. "And I plan to leave the energy containment canister on board, too."

"Of course," Janeway said, smiling.

"It will be done in fifty seconds," B'Elanna said.

"Won't they just blow the yacht apart the minute it leaves our shields?" Kim asked.

"Let's hope not," Janeway said. "I'm betting none of them want to be the one to destroy their prince's yacht."

"So it will blow up right in the center of them?" Chakotay said. "Great idea."

"We can hope," Janeway said. "Otherwise we might as well just toss shoes at them, for all the good this is going to do us."

"Thirty seconds," B'Elanna's voice echoed over the bridge.

"Everyone's doing countdowns," Tom said, shaking his head in disgust.

"Hail the Qavok warships," Janeway said. "Audio only."

"Ready, Captain," Kim said just as another volley of phaser shots rocked *Voyager*.

"Qavok warriors," Janeway said. "Our society honors its greatest warriors with prizes and awards. You have fought well this day. We honor you by returning your prince's yacht to you as we promised. Before our final battle."

She cut the connection.

"Think they bought it?" Chakotay asked.

"I don't know," Janeway said. "But at least they can't say I don't keep my promises."

Tom laughed, shaking his head at her lame joke.

"Shuttle launching," B'Elanna said. "Explosive time set for thirty seconds. Mark. Now."

"Tom," Janeway said. "Please tell me we still have impulse power."

He glanced around at her and smiled. "We still have impulse, Captain. And warp for that matter."

"Then take us and put us between the coming explosion and the shuttle. As close to the shuttle as you can get, just in case they don't have enough screens."

"As if we do," Ensign Kim said. "We're holding at twenty-six percent."

"Now, Tom," she said. "Get us out of here."

On the screen the yacht drifted toward the Qavok warships and the bomb ship in their center.

Tom swung *Voyager* wide and accelerated to the shuttle, turning so that they faced the Qavok warships, which were now out of range.

"Fifteen seconds," Chakotay said.

"Get us more screens," Janeway ordered.

"Doing my best, Captain," Kim said.

"They're going for it," Chakotay said.

"Lucky for us they never read about the Trojan horse," Tom said.

"I've established a link with the shuttle," Kim said.

"Tuvok," Janeway said.

"Yes, Captain," Tuvok's voice came back clear.

"Your shield situation?"

"We have almost thirty percent," he said.

"Okay," she said. "Hold on to something. This may get a little rough at this distance."

"Captain?" She could picture him raising a questioning eyebrow.

"You'll understand in a few seconds. Just hold on."

The yacht was being pulled toward one warship with a tractor beam. Two warships were escorting the bomb ship past the yacht toward its appointed time of reckoning with the neutron star binary.

Janeway held her breath. If that yacht didn't blow up, the only thing standing between the destruction of the Lekk homeworld and safety was a Xorm science ship.

"Five," Ensign Kim said.

"Four."

"Three."

"I hate this," Tom said.

"Two."

"Everyone brace yourselves," Janeway ordered, her voice going out over the entire ship.

"One."

"Now."

The main screen flashed white.

Blinding white.

Pure white.

A flash so bright that even the instant filters didn't catch enough of the light to stop it from hurting Janeway's eyes.

Then the shock wave hit.

Hard.

It seemed as if a giant hand had grabbed the bridge and simply tipped it up on end.

Janeway tumbled over the back of her chair and rolled hard into the step, knocking the wind out of her lungs and sending stars spinning through her head.

The lights flickered and then for a moment went out. Then they came back on just as fast.

The noise was like the worst earthquake, rumbling and deep, filling every space, moving through the floor around her.

And then, as quickly as it hit, it passed.

The light was normal, the noise gone.

Her shoulder and head hurt, but not enough to keep her on the floor.

She pulled herself to her feet and stared at the main screen. The binary was still there, of course. But the entire Qavok fleet was gone. Shattered and vaporized.

"Everyone all right?" she said, turning to look at the bridge crew.

Kim was back at his post and Chakotay was climbing slowly to his feet. Everyone was alive.

"Captain," Tuvok's voice came over the com line clearly. "We're going to need medical assistance here. Dr. Maalot has been injured."

Janeway glanced around at Kim. "Are the transporters still working?"

"One hundred percent, Captain," Kim said.

"Beam Dr. Maalot to sickbay at once. Warn the Doctor."

"I'm sure after that hit," Chakotay said, "he's got a lot to do."

Janeway only nodded. She was staring at where the fleet of Qavok warships had been. Now only empty space.

She dropped down into her chair. She could really use a cup of coffee. But first things first.

"Ensign, open a channel to the Xorm. Let's see if they survived."

"On screen," Kim said.

"Brilliant, Captain," Fedr said, his smiling face filling the screen.

"Did you ride the explosion all right?"

"Actually," he said, "since we were below and our orbit was off to one side slightly, we felt very little. The intense energy coming off the binary seemed to block most of the force."

"Good," she said. "Anything we can do for you?"

"Not at the moment, Captain," Fedr said. "I think we'll just hold this position for a time and continue our study."

Janeway nodded, staring at the other captain for a moment. Something felt wrong, but at the moment her headache didn't let her doubts through. And for the life of her, she couldn't put her finger on it.

"Very good," she said. "We'll also stay and do repairs, then watch the explosion from a safe distance."

"Again, Captain," Fedr said. "My compliments on dealing with the Qavok. They are really evil and your solution was truly brilliant."

His smile flickered and then he cut the connection.

"Weird," Tom said.

Janeway glanced at her pilot. "How is that?"

"Why would they stay in that orbit when they can get almost the exact same information at a higher and safer orbit?"

She sat back, forcing the throbbing from the bump on her head into the background. Staying at that low, very dangerous orbit didn't make any sense. There was no reason to go that low into the binary unless—

She stood. Of course. Why hadn't she seen what was going on before now?

"Okay," she said. "Listen up, people. We have work to do and we're going to have to do it fast if we're going to hit our deadline."

"What deadline?" Tom asked.

"The deadline to stop that neutron star from plowing through inhabited systems."

"That deadline is only minutes away," Chakotay said. "We can't make that one, Captain."

"I know, but I'm betting we have a second window."

"Captain," Kim said. "We blew up the yacht, remember?"

"Oh, I remember," she said, laughing and gently touching the bump on the back of her head. The pain was declining, but unless she got down to sickbay soon, she was going to have one heck of a headache. That didn't matter. She didn't have time for that now.

She had a neutron star to send safely out of the galaxy.

CHAPTER 21

"SEVEN?" CAPTAIN JANEWAY'S HAIL FILLED THE ENGI-neering section of *Voyager*. Seven of Nine was there, working on repairs to the phasers. She considered it simple work. Necessary to the safety of the entire ship, thus important.

"Yes, Captain," she said.

"I need you to run a few very quick calculations for me," Janeway said.

"Certainly," Seven said. She moved over to a console and prepared it. "Go ahead."

"Are you familiar with the size of the warp core on a Qavok warship?"

"I have the specifications," Seven said. She quickly brought up the newly entered specs taken from the yacht's computer, and displayed them on the screen.

"Using the power generated with a warp-core breach of a Qavok warship core," Janeway said, talking slowly, clearly to make sure she was understood, "would it be possible to alter the path of the neutron star to the safe path out of the galaxy?"

"One moment," Seven said.

Her fingers keyed in the data and ran the formulas. She had run this type of calculation so many times over the past hours, she almost knew it well enough to figure it without the help of the computer. Yet, to guarantee that she gave the captain the correct data, she used the computer. The result a few seconds later agreed with her initial estimate.

"Yes, Captain," she said. "The warp-core breach of that magnitude would have to be in an exact location above the secondary neutron star, but it could be done."

"How soon?" Janeway said.

"Twenty-six minutes, ten seconds," Seven said. "The difference in time from our previous estimate is, of course, the result of the difference in size of the energy generated by a core breach of that size."

"Understood," Janeway said. "I was hoping that would be the case. Now, one more quick calculation if you would."

"Certainly."

"Do you have the coordinates for the Qavok home system?" Janeway asked.

"I do," Seven said, her fingers moving as she spoke to pull up the information on her board.

"Figure, using the same size core, what it would take to send the neutron star through the Qavok home system. And when such a change would need to be made?"

"Captain?" Seven said. Certainly Captain Janeway was not thinking of sending the neutron star through an inhabited system.

"Do it, please," Janeway said. Her voice was cold and to the point.

Seven ran the numbers quickly.

"It would be possible," Seven said.

"When?"

Seven glanced at her calculations. "Eighteen minutes."

Seven heard Janeway sigh, then there was silence.

"Captain?" Seven said.

"Sorry," Janeway said. "Just thinking. I need you to stop what you were doing and double- and triple-check your calculations for sending the neutron star out of the galaxy safely. That way, if we have success dealing with the other side of this equation, we'll be ready."

"I'm afraid," Seven said, "that I do not follow you."

"You will," Janeway said. "Just double-check those figures. If we try sending that neutron star out of the galaxy, I don't want any mistakes. Understood?"

"Perfectly," Seven said.

Janeway cut the connection. For a moment Seven stood, staring at the two calculations she had done for the captain. Then she cleared the second one and went to work double-checking the first. There were many details that had to be considered. She would consider them all.

The tractor beam settled the shuttle safely onto the shuttlebay deck with a slight thump. Tyla sat silent for a moment in the copilot's chair as beside her Tuvok shut down the last of the shuttle systems.

After he was finished, she said, "Thank you for allowing us to help."

Tuvok nodded. "You were logical choices."

Tyla smiled.

She climbed from the chair and a few moments later was heading down the hallway toward sickbay. She'd been with Dr. Maalot so long, she was actually starting to like the physicist. And when the shock wave had sent him against that bulkhead and knocked him unconscious, she was worried for his safety.

Very worried.

Then suddenly he had disappeared from the shuttle—"beamed," as they put it, to sickbay. And at that moment she understood, finally, how she had been so easily captured during her stupid escape attempt.

A dozen people were sitting on the floor of the sickbay, holding an arm or a bandaged leg, apparently waiting their turn. The few beds were full and a bald-headed human was efficiently moving around the tables.

"Please state the nature of your medical emergency," he said, glancing up at her as she entered.

"Just here to check on the condition of Dr. Maalot," she said. "I am not injured."

"Well," the Doctor said, "thank you for that." He shook his head in seeming amazement, then pointed over his shoulder. "He's on the first bed. Nothing serious."

Tyla felt a sense of relief at that news.

She moved over to where Dr. Maalot lay, his eyes closed. As she approached, he smiled weakly. "Thanks for coming to check up on me, Lieutenant."

"We've been together too long now to have something happen this close to the end."

"Did we stop the Qavok?"

"Completely," Tyla said, smiling. "Captain Janeway sent the prince's yacht right into the middle of them, set to blow up." She loved the irony of that solution.

Dr. Maalot sat up, looking almost shocked. "With the energy container on board?"

Tyla nodded, still smiling. "None of the Qavok captains wanted to get in trouble by destroying their prince's yacht. Janeway just floated it right out into the middle of them, hailed them to tell them it was their reward, and then blew it up. Wonderful, just wonderful."

Maalot laughed, then moaned and lay back down, still smiling. "It seems," he said, "that your stealing the yacht saved our planet."

Tyla stopped smiling. She didn't like the idea of being considered any sort of hero. She had simply been doing her job.

Dr. Maalot didn't seem to notice her change of mood. He just went on. "It's just too bad that now Janeway won't be able to trigger the exploding neutron star and get its primary companion out of the galaxy safely. Too bad for a number of worlds along the way."

Tyla suddenly found herself thinking of those worlds. There were millions on those worlds who would have made a different decision today. Saving their own worlds would have come first over saving another. Just as saving the Lekk homeworld had been her first priority.

"The Doctor says I should be up in fifteen minutes. Where will I be able to find you?"

Tyla shrugged. "I guess I'll ask Captain Janeway if I can watch the neutron star binary explosion from the bridge."

"I would like that," he said. "Would you ask for me, also?"

"I'd be glad to." She patted his arm. "Now you rest until the Doctor tells you to move."

"Young woman," the Doctor said to Tyla, "I wish more of my patients were as smart as you."

"He's the smart one," she said, pointing at Maalot. "I'm just a soldier."

The Doctor only grunted and went back to work.

She moved out into the hall, and suddenly, for the first time in a while, she realized she was hungry. Maybe the strange man, Neelix, would be able to find her some food. She had time.

Or at least she thought she did.

"Captain Janeway to Lieutenant Tyla. Would you please report to the bridge?"

The question froze her in midstep. She glanced around, but couldn't see what to do. She had seen the crew tap their badges and reply, but she didn't have a badge. Another crew member—a young-looking man with short brown hair—was in the hall nearby.

"Excuse me," Tyla said. "I'm Lieutenant Tyla. How do I respond to the captain?"

The guy smiled and pointed at the wall. "Right there. Tap it once and speak. The computer will get it to the right place."

"Thank you."

She quickly tapped the button. "Lieutenant Tyla here. On my way."

"Thank you," Janeway said.

Tyla nodded and stepped back, almost bumping into the crew member who had stayed to make sure she didn't need any more help.

"Sorry," he said. "You know it isn't often many of us get called to the bridge."

Tyla smiled. "That's all right," she said. "I'm just a guest. There aren't many of you lucky enough to be on *Voyager.*"

He nodded, clearly thinking about what she had

said as she turned away and headed for the bridge at a fast walk.

She really did feel that any crew member of this wonderful craft was lucky. And if she didn't have so much information about the Qavok to take home, she would be tempted to ask to stay on board.

But not this time.

CHAPTER
22

Janeway ended the brief conversation with Lieutenant Tyla and glanced around the bridge at her crew. They were all staring at her, the joy of surviving the Qavok attack suddenly forgotten after hearing her exchange with Seven.

Lieutenant Tyla entered the bridge, and Janeway motioned that she take a position next to Tuvok. Torres came in behind her by a few steps.

Good.

"Here's what I'm thinking," Janeway said. "I believe that in about sixteen to eighteen minutes the Xorm ship *Gravity* will send a warp core down at the binary, in an attempt to shift the neutron star onto a path through the Qavok home system."

"What?" Chakotay said.

Tyla looked suddenly ill.

"Is that possible?" the first officer asked.

Janeway nodded. "Seven did the initial math, but yes it is, using a standard warp core found on Xorm and Qavok ships."

"And you think they're carrying a second active warp core?" Chakotay asked.

"Actually," Janeway said, "this is only a suspicion. Lieutenant Tyla, what can you tell us about the Xorm? So far we've been taking them at face value."

Tyla shrugged. "There's not much to say. They have been at war with the Qavok for centuries, but over all of my lifetime, they have never actually fought. They both worked for my homeworld to join their side, and when we opted to stay neutral, the Qavok invaded."

"Do you think the Xorm are capable of doing such a terrible thing?"

Again Tyla only shrugged. "I would imagine that anything is possible. The Xorm are smarter than the Qavok, but less military. If the Qavok thought of a way to send the star into our homeworld, I'm sure the Xorm thought of a way of using it against the Qavok. That would solve their perennial Qavok issue permanently."

"All right," Janeway said, "so we can't rule out the possibility. I'm afraid we must progress under the assumption that they are going to try it."

"Captain, if you'll pardon me," Kim said, "but I'm still not following."

"Tom?" Janeway asked, turning to her pilot.

"Nobody in their right mind would stay in that low orbit for observation," Tom replied. "There's nothing they can get there that they can't get at a higher orbit. Therefore, it only makes sense to conclude that they wanted to stay that close for reasons other than research."

Kim nodded. "Got it."

"B'Elanna," Janeway said, "any chance of weapons anytime soon?"

"Not for hours," she said. "Sorry."

"We'll just have to think of other options."

"Captain," Tuvok said. "The shuttle still has weapons capability."

"But no power?"

"Correct."

"Well, we still may be able to use those weapons. Get back down to the shuttlebay and stand by. Lieutenant Tyla, would you go with him?"

"Pleasure," she said.

"Okay, people," Janeway said, "red alert. Battle stations. I want everything ready if we need to move."

The red lights came and the battle stations sounded. Tuvok and Tyla ducked out the door at a fast walk. Chakotay stepped back into Tuvok's position.

Janeway sat down in her command chair. "Tom, ease us down toward the Xorm."

"Aye, Captain," he said. "It might get a little rough."

"Just as long as we survive," she said.

"No problem there," he said.

"Mr. Kim, Chakotay, I want full scans of the Xorm ship. Look for a second active warp core. If there isn't one, we'll apologize, back out of here, and go to Plan B."

"They're trying to block our scans, Captain," Kim said after a moment. "But they're not succeeding," he continued with a note of triumph.

"Got it," Chakotay said. "On their shuttle deck, inside a small ship of some kind."

Janeway glanced around at her second-in-command just as he looked up. "It's in an unmanned shuttle."

"And it's not the shuttle's power source and drive?"

"No," Chakotay said. "It's baggage. Nothing more."

"Damn," she said. "I was hoping I was wrong."

"So was I, Captain," Tom said. "No offense."

"None taken."

"The Xorm are hailing us."

"On screen," Janeway said, taking a deep breath and forcing herself to look stern.

"What is the meaning of scanning us, Captain?" Fedr said, his eyes nothing more than slits.

"Well," Janeway said, acting calmly, "when you decided to stay at such a low orbit, I got to wondering why."

Captain Fedr's face slowly grew slightly red. "As I said. Research on the binary."

"Would you care to explain to me what information you can get in that extremely dangerous and difficult-to-maintain orbit that you could not get at, say, the location we are at now?"

Janeway just kept smiling. She wanted to make sure she didn't shove him in the wrong way.

Captain Fedr's face just kept getting redder and redder.

"With all due respect, Captain, that is our business and not yours."

"Ahh, I see," Janeway said, now no longer smiling. "You're not planning, by chance, to use the extra warp core in your shuttlebay to send the neutron star at the Qavok homeworld?"

"With due respect, I am simply following my orders. This discussion has ended," Fedr said ruefully.

The connection was terminated and the spinning neutron star binary filled the screen.

"Guess we got the answer we needed," she said. "Not the one we wanted, though."

Behind her the bridge was deathly silent.

She tapped her combadge. "Seven?"

"Go ahead, Captain."

"We found an extra warp core on the Xorm ship. Harry's loading the information our scans got down to you. What I need to know is how much time we have before they launch it."

"I will have the answer in a moment, Captain," Seven said.

Janeway glanced back at Chakotay. "Any chance we can transport through their shields?"

Chakotay did a quick check of the board in front of him, then shook his head. "Afraid not."

"Too bad," Janeway said. "That would have made it so easy."

"Captain," Seven said. "Taking all factors into account, including the time it will take for the warp core to reach the desired height above the secondary neutron star, the time remaining is nine minutes and ten seconds. Mark."

"Got it," Kim said.

"Thanks. Keep working on the second time frame," Janeway told Seven. "I'm hoping we're going to get a chance to use it."

"Understood," Seven said.

"All right, I'm open to suggestions here."

"The shuttle is the answer, Captain," Chakotay said.

"How?"

"We hold it outside our screens with a tractor beam, let it fire enough to knock down the Xorm shields. When they're down, we'll beam that warp core out of the Xorm ship and destroy it."

"Without shields, Captain," Tom said, "the Xorm ship won't last long in that orbit."

Janeway nodded. "Unfortunately, that's their problem. Unless someone has a better idea, I'm going with this one."

"Captain," B'Elanna said. "We could have the shuttle blow up the warp core right after it has launched and is outside the Xorm shields."

Janeway nodded. A second good idea. "We'll

hold that as our backup in case the first plan doesn't work. That's cutting things just a little too close for my taste. Other suggestions?"

Nothing.

"All right then, let's do it. B'Elanna, I want you down there running the tractor beam. Make it solid, double it up where you can. This is going to be a bumpy ride and we don't want to lose them."

"Got it," she said, and headed for the door.

"Tuvok," Janeway said on the comm line. "Here's what we're going to try to do."

It took her less than a minute to explain the plan. That left seven minutes and thirty seconds to put it all in motion.

Seven minutes to slowly count down. She desperately needed a cup of coffee.

And maybe about seven hours of sleep.

CHAPTER
23

"LAUNCH THE SHUTTLE," JANEWAY SAID.

"Launching," B'Elanna said.

"Three minutes, ten seconds remaining," Harry said.

On the screen, the beautiful shape of the Xorm ship *Gravity* floated between *Voyager* and the binary neutron star. The binary was now spinning off so much mass, it looked more like a swirling spiral galaxy to Janeway than a binary star. And there was no way to tell the two stars apart anymore with the naked eye. They were both just one big blur on the main screen. Very shortly, just before the final moment, the binary period would decrease to barely six milliseconds.

Voyager jolted and Janeway held on to the arm of

her command chair. They were back at their original orbit level. The Xorm ship was below them a considerable distance, but within easy phaser range.

"Rougher than just an hour before, Captain," Tom said. "I have no idea how the Xorm ship is holding that orbit."

"Just keep us right here," Janeway said. "And we'll soon find out just how stable they are."

"Shuttle in position," B'Elanna said.

"Xorm powering weapons," Ensign Kim said.

"Extra power to forward shields," Janeway said.

"Shields at sixty-five percent," Chakotay said.

A greenish beam shot out of the Xorm ship and lit up *Voyager*'s front shield. Janeway was snapped back hard, but managed to stay in her chair. For a moment the lights dimmed, then came back up.

"Shields at fifty percent," Chakotay said. "Almost no damage."

"More punch than the Qavok," Janeway said. "But that sure answers any question as to their intent, doesn't it."

"That it does," Chakotay said.

"Tom, bring us around so the shuttle is in firing position."

"Aye, Captain."

Right now the shuttle, held by a tractor beam, was like an outrigger off the side of *Voyager*. Or, more accurately, a giant weapon held away from the body of the ship.

"Coming around now," Tom said.

"Fire when you are clear, Mr. Tuvok," Janeway said.

"Firing now."

Two phaser beams shot out, sending the Xorm ship's shields into the dark reds.

"Their shields are holding," Kim said.

Janeway was afraid of that. For some reason she knew the Xorm were really more powerful technologically than the Qavok. More than likely, the Qavok simply overpowered them by sheer numbers centuries before, as they had tried to do today.

"Fire again, Mr. Tuvok."

Before he could fire, the Xorm ship fired first, smashing a green-tinted beam into *Voyager* like a massive fist.

This time Janeway was knocked sideways, up and out of her chair to her right. She hit hard, but rolled quickly and came up on one knee. She would have a bruise on the shoulder tomorrow.

"Status of the shuttle?"

"One tractor beam is down," B'Elanna said. "Still got the shuttle by another."

"Don't lose them," Janeway said.

Losing the shuttle without power this close to the binary would be like losing a child's float in a fast-moving river headed for a waterfall. There was very little chance they'd recover it if they didn't get it quickly.

"Firing," Tuvok said, his voice filling the bridge.

Two more phaser shots cut at the Xorm screens.

"They're damaged," Kim said. "They have some shield damage and fires throughout their ship."

"Can you get a lock on that warp core?" Chakotay asked.

"Got it," Kim said.

"Beam it out of there into space and strip the containment away so it explodes away from the neutron star binary," Janeway said.

"Done," Kim said.

A white light lit up the screen like a small sun suddenly coming into being, then quickly faded.

Again the Xorm fired.

Voyager rocked hard.

"Oh, we made them mad," Paris said.

"Screens at twenty percent," Chakotay said. "And we've lost the shuttle. I've got a position lock on them. The shuttle's orbit is being destabilized."

"Grab it, B'Elanna," Janeway said.

"That last shot knocked all tractor systems off-line," B'Elanna said. "I'm working on it."

"Ensign, get a transporter lock on them and make sure you keep it locked."

"Understood," Kim said.

"Tuvok," Janeway said. "Hang on and we'll retrieve you."

"We have little choice," Tuvok said.

Janeway nodded. She knew he was right. There was no choice as far as he was concerned.

None at all.

* * *

Not many hours—yet a lifetime ago—Lieutenant Tyla had tried to steal this shuttle. Now she was being trusted to help fly it for the second time. Her pride and Captain Janeway's faith in her made her want to do the best job possible.

The shots she had fired had hit their mark on the Xorm ship. It was the first time in her entire career that she had ever fired on a Xorm ship. And it was to save the homeworld of the Qavok—her most hated enemy. Her view of life had certainly changed since she was rescued by *Voyager*.

Changed completely.

The Xorm shot against the *Voyager* shields had jarred the shuttle like a child shaking a rattle. She and Tuvok somehow had managed to stay in their seats, but not by much. She had banged her shoulder hard, but was ignoring the pain for the moment.

Now, after another shot from the Xorm ship, they were loose from *Voyager*. The tractor beams had released them.

And she knew there was very little hope of salvation. The shuttle was bobbing and shaking along due to the rapidly changing gravitational field of the binary orbital motion as if it were a raft in a whitewater-filled river.

"Tuvok," she said, staring at the screens. "Do we have any attitude thrusters still available? Enough to turn us slightly?"

"Yes," Tuvok said. "We do. But they will not have much effect in this turbulence."

"If you can get us turned, I think I might be able to get a computer lock on the Xorm ship from here. Our phasers are still at eighty percent."

"An interesting thought," he said. "Captain, there is a possibility that we would be able to continue to fire at the Xorm vessel."

"Do it," Janeway said.

Tuvok's fingers flew over the controls and the shuttle turned slowly. On the panel in front of her she saw the image of the Xorm ship come into view. Slowly, moving toward the targeting area of the screen.

Her fingers worked the controls, trying to get the computer to lock on to the Xorm ship even with the rough, up-and-down ride the forces off the binary were handing them.

Then the lock grabbed and held green. "Got them."

Then it was lost again.

"Fire," Tuvok said.

"Lost lock," she said.

"Fire manually," he said. "I will attempt to steady the ship as best I can."

She couldn't tell the difference. She was going to have to fire soon.

She led the drift, watching it. Up. Down. Sideways then back up.

She watched the pattern, knew when the ship was coming back on target. Then, just as the Xorm ship was to pass through the target, she fired.

The phaser lit up the Xorm's remaining screens,

then cut through the body of the ship, leaving a wide gash.

"They won't be firing at *Voyager* anymore," Tyla said.

"A direct hit under these conditions is admirable," Tuvok said calmly.

"Thank you," she said.

As they watched, the Xorm warship lost control of its orbit, got too close to the neutron stars at its periastron passage, and was torn apart in an explosion of white light.

And Tyla knew that in a few seconds, after a very rough ride, that would be their fate.

"Xorm ship destroyed," Kim said.

Janeway permitted herself a sigh of relief. But only a small one. At least they wouldn't be fired on anymore. Now all they had to deal with was a neutron star explosion in the binary.

"Stay with the shuttle, Tom."

"Right with them," Tom said. "Like a big brother."

"You still have a transporter lock on the crew, Mr. Kim?" Janeway asked.

"Got them solidly," Kim said. "No problems."

Voyager was bucking in the incredible variable gravitational forces coming off the neutron binary. It felt as if the entire ship was being torn apart around her. Janeway doubted they could take much more. She had no idea how Tuvok and Tyla were managing on the shuttle.

"At periastron, we're approaching the same distance the Xorm ship was."

"How much time do we have before the shuttle goes too low at its periastron?" Janeway asked.

"Less than ten seconds," Chakotay said.

"Get ready to get them out of there, Mr. Kim," she said.

"Ready, Captain."

"B'Elanna?" Janeway said. "No time left."

"Tractor beams coming back on-line now, Captain."

"Got them," Chakotay said.

"Tom, pull us up out of here."

"Gladly," he said.

"Slowly," she said. "We don't want to lose the shuttle a second time."

Tom nodded and for the next few seconds *Voyager* continued to rattle and shake as Tom moved them up away from the intense, rapidly changing gravity well of the binary.

"Tuvok? Lieutenant Tyla?" Janeway asked. "Are you all right?"

"Bruised," Tuvok said. "But otherwise our health is fine. I am pleased we could save the shuttle."

"So am I," she said.

Tom let out a deep sigh and leaned back, sweat dripping from his neck and staining the back of his shirt.

Janeway sat back in her command chair for a

moment and stared at the binary on the main screen. It was lucky there weren't more of these things in the galaxy. They were too dangerous. Far too dangerous.

Then she stood.

There was still one more task to accomplish.

A few more worlds to save.

CHAPTER
24

IN ALL HIS YEARS OF COMMAND, CAPTAIN QADOS OF the Qavok warship *Invincible* had never had such a bad day.

Never.

Around him his crew worked intently. And very silently, not daring to speak. The smoke still filled the air of his command, forcing his second eyelids down, making everything seem blurry. The smell of burning equipment choked him, but he did not allow himself to cough and show weakness. He would remain strong and in command until the very end. And if they escaped, he would become the hero of this fight. The only ship to survive against the dreaded humans.

The human ship *Voyager,* with its insufferable

Captain Janeway, had destroyed their shields, their weapons, and their drives. Only the skill of Command Pilot Qaad had kept them orbiting the neutron star on maneuvering thrusters. They were just barely holding an orbit, but unable to pull away at all.

Unless they got their warp drive back on-line very soon, it would make no difference. They would be vaporized when the neutron star exploded.

The ship hit a bump, as if it had just run over something on a smooth road. Normally he would have yelled at any pilot who made such a mistake, but Command Pilot Qaad was doing his best under these trying conditions and Qados knew it. No amount of yelling would help at this point anyway.

The worst part of the day was the moment the *Voyager* captain had tricked his proud Qavok fleet into taking the prince's yacht back. Of course it had been a trap. Why else would a monster like Janeway send out such a gift? Surely not out of goodwill. He would have tried to warn his comrades, but he was on the other side of the binary at that moment. There was nothing he could have done.

They were stupid.

They deserved to die.

Now, over the last few minutes, he had sat, mouth slightly open, teeth partially exposed, as *Voyager* obliterated the Xorm ship.

At first he had wondered if there was no satisfying this human captain's desire to destroy. He could see no reason why the human ship should challenge the Xorm. But then his communications officer had intercepted a conversation between the Xorm captain and Janeway.

It then became clear that Captain Janeway was now defending the Qavok homeworld from Xorm attempt to alter the neutron star's path. It had not occurred to Qados that the Xorm would even try such a thing. Yet, in hindsight, he should have expected it. Such a monstrous thing was in the Xorm nature.

"Captain," his communications officer said, using the signal of complete subservience. *"Voyager* approaches. Hails us."

"On the main," Qados said. He stood and stepped forward, so that Captain Janeway could not see the destruction behind him. No point in letting an enemy know any more than they needed to know. Even though this enemy had just defended his homeworld.

"Captain Janeway," Qados said as the pale, sickly human face of the captain appeared on the screen. "Your actions in defense of the Qavok homeworld have been noted."

"Good," Janeway said. "Then you won't mind my taking your ship, will you? We need to run a few errands."

"What?"

"I have no time to debate," she said, baring her teeth at him. "Stand by. You will be held in a safe place until we can transport you to the Lekk homeworld, where they will do with you as they please."

"We will fight to the death to defend our ship," Qados said.

Janeway just sighed and cut the connection.

"Stand ready to be boarded," he shouted.

At that moment the bridge around him started to shimmer, as if he were looking at it through three eyelids instead of two.

Then it faded to black.

He opened all four eyelids, but it remained black for that instant.

Then around him a new room shimmered into being. Metal walls, and a damaged shuttle sitting on one side of the room. Ten humans with weapons stood around the area where he had appeared.

He, *and* the rest of his crew.

All without weapons.

He patted his chest, searching for his gun to cut the humans down. His guns were also gone.

He roared and charged the closest guard.

Only to smash hard into a forcefield and go down on his back.

His third eyelid closed, then his fourth.

And around him the nightmare faded to black.

"Got them all," Kim said, looking up and smiling.

"Mr. Tuvok, are the prisoners contained?"

"They are, Captain," he said, his voice coming clear through the comm from the shuttle deck.

"But it seems we have violated a cultural taboo by depriving them of weapons. They are cowering in corners."

"Wait until the Lekks get ahold of them," Janeway said. "I have a sneaking hunch this will seem minor."

Near the door to the bridge Lieutenant Tyla nodded and smiled.

"I agree," Tuvok said.

"How much time do we have, Mr. Kim?" Janeway asked, turning her attention away from the thought of over a hundred cowering lizards and back to the task at hand.

"Using the Qavok warp core, five minutes and ten seconds."

"Tyla," Janeway said, "think you can fly a Qavok warship on thrusters, at least well enough to send it down into that binary?"

"I would gladly sacrifice my life to do so," Tyla said, her face firm, her back straight.

"I have no intention of sacrificing your life," Janeway said, making sure she did not smile. "Or mine. I'm going along with you."

Lieutenant Tyla looked puzzled, but said nothing.

"Transporter," Harry whispered. "Remember?"

Lieutenant Tyla's face brightened and she nodded.

Janeway tapped the comm. "Seven, are you ready?"

"Standing by," Seven said.

"Mr. Kim," Janeway said. "We have no time to go to the transporter room. Site-to-site transfer. Put us on the bridge of the *Invincible* and keep a computer lock on us at all times."

"Understood."

"You have the bridge, Commander," Janeway said.

She smiled at the worried look on her second-in-command's face, then said, "Energize."

B'Elanna crawled under the panel in Engineering and stared at the smoking mess that faced her. All warp-drive controls and backups had been fried. Normally this would take a day to fix. She had just an hour and not one second longer before the neutron star explosion itself.

She climbed back to her feet and pounded her fist on the panel. "Damn." She tapped her comm badge. "All engineering staff report on the double. Drop everything you are doing and get here."

She glanced around at the others staring at her. Then she turned and yanked off the cover of the panel, digging into the burnt and fused wires. No point in waiting for help. Every second was going to count if this was going to be fixed.

And they didn't have too many seconds left.

A moment after she had been standing on the bridge of *Voyager*, the transport beam reassembled Janeway's molecules on the bridge of the *Invincible*, beside the captain's stained chair.

She glanced around through the smoke-filled room, crowded with equipment. The floor was covered in garbage and equipment, seemingly discarded at random over a period of time.

She took a shallow breath and then coughed. "What a smell."

"Qavok are known for their unsanitary living conditions," Tyla said.

Janeway laughed, then coughed again. It was going to take ten showers to get this smell out of her hair and off her skin.

"Controls." She pointed at one set of panels.

Tyla nodded and moved over and sat down in the large chair. She studied the panel for only a moment, then gently played her hand across the board, firing a port-side thruster just enough to right the course and keep the orbit stable.

Seven finished studying the inside of the ship with a recorder. "The Qavok would be ignored by the Borg," she said. "Nothing to offer the Collective."

Janeway laughed, somehow without breathing.

Seven stood behind Tyla and studied the panel, then leaned forward and keyed some numbers into the controls beside Tyla. "The coordinates. We must arrive in precisely three minutes and seventeen seconds from this mark. Not one millisecond early or late."

"Understood," Tyla said.

Janeway watched as the young Lekk pilot slowly

moved the Qavok warship around and nudged it in the right direction with only a few bumps.

"Nice," Janeway said. "Keep us on track."

"Janeway to *Voyager*. We're set here and moving. Should have brought air tanks, but otherwise we're fine. Follow us down at a safe distance."

Chakotay's voice came back clear and strong. *"Voyager* here. Understood, except we have a slight problem. B'Elanna hasn't gotten warp drive back on-line yet and Tom's a little hesitant to go too low with only thrusters and impulse. Afraid we might not be able to pull safely out of the gravity well."

"Understood," Janeway said. "Just pace us and stay close enough to keep a transporter lock on us in case this goes bad."

"Will do," Chakotay said. "Out."

Janeway moved down and stood over Tyla's right shoulder. Seven looked up at her with a raised eyebrow. "Warp drive is out?"

"Yes," Janeway said. "I know, I know."

Without warp, they were in the process of speeding up their own deaths by exactly two point three nine milliseconds.

CHAPTER
25

CHAKOTAY MOVED OVER AND STOOD NEXT TO ENSIGN Kim, just in case he needed any help with the transporter. There was no way he was going to lose Kathryn, Seven, and Tyla at this point.

"Everything is functioning, Commander," Kim said. "Transporter lock is solid on all three."

"Good," he said. But he didn't move away. He just felt better being where the action was.

On the big screen the Qavok warship flashed across as an ungainly blemish against the backdrop of the beautiful, swirling binary. Unlike the Xorm ship, there was nothing good-looking at all about a Qavok warship.

"Three minutes for beam-out from *Invincible*," Kim said.

"Another countdown," Tom said. "We're going for a countdown record today."

"Seems that way, doesn't it?" Chakotay said.

Voyager jolted slightly and Tom shook his head. "They must be getting pounded over there."

"They're still on course," Kim said. "And on time."

"You just keep your eye on that transport lock, mister," Chakotay said. "I'll watch their progress."

"Yes, sir," Kim said. "Would you like me to keep announcing the countdown?"

Tom sighed. Heavily.

As B'Elanna's entire engineering staff poured in, she quickly gave them their jobs. They were going to attack the problem from every side possible. They were going to go after any chance of getting the warp drives running again. Any chance at all.

One team was going to try to fix the main systems. Their prognosis wasn't good. But they were going to try.

A second team was going to try to fix the backup system. Those components had less damage and the team stood a decent chance of finishing it.

Yet a third team, which she would head, was going to try to build an entire new bypass control system for warp drive. If they were lucky they'd manage to jump the ship into warp long enough to outrun the leading edge of the neutron-star explosion. B'Elanna gave this option the best chance of success. And when Janeway and Seven returned, they could chip in and help. Every hand was going to be needed to save them this time.

"One hour, people," B'Elanna barked as she banged her fist on an uncooperative control panel.

Janeway felt as if she were riding a bucking steer. What stabilizers the Qavok ship had seemed to have were off-line. Seven yanked a cord belt tight over Tyla's lap to hold her in her seat. Under different circumstances Janeway might have praised the former Borg's very human improvisation. But now was not the time.

Janeway gripped a pipe just to stay on her feet and envied Seven's balance.

"One minute to beam-out point," Chakotay said.

"We are falling slightly too fast," Seven said.

"Compensating," Tyla said, her voice terse. "The thrusters can only slow us down so much against this gravity."

"Understood," Seven said. "I've compensated for such acceleration after we've beamed out. But we must slow down exactly by sixty-four kilometers per second in the next thirty seconds."

"I'm not sure if the forward thrusters have that kind of strength," Tyla said.

"How about the aft thrusters?" Janeway asked.

Tyla nodded. "There are four of them, all working," she said.

"Do you have time to turn the ship?"

"I do," Tyla said.

"That will affect the final few seconds of the flight, but I will compensate," Seven said, busy working out the math.

"Hold on," Tyla said. "When I turn the ship sideways, it will get very rough."

"Holding," Janeway said.

"Turning," Tyla said.

She wasn't kidding when she said it was going to get rough. It felt like the room had rotated upward a full ninety degrees. Janeway knew that if they survived this, the doctor was going to have to take a whole bunch of bumps to task.

"Everything all right?" Chakotay's voice filled the Qavok bridge.

"Fine, Commander," Janeway said. "We just needed to take the ship in aft first. Better resistance."

"Understood," he said. "Thirty seconds."

"There," Seven said. "We are again on the correct course and on time."

Janeway held her breath, waiting, watching her two crew members accomplish the seemingly impossible task of flying an alien warship into a neutron star binary with only thrusters. Janeway just wished that she could see the space outside of the ship, the binary, the matter swirling off of it. Then again, maybe it was better she couldn't at the moment.

"Fifteen seconds," Chakotay's voice again echoed through the bridge.

"Pull back slightly," Seven said, watching her instruments.

Tyla's hands flew over the controls. The woman was one fine pilot. Maybe almost as good as Tom.

Again the ship bucked and rolled. Janeway managed to hold on to the pipe as her feet flew out from under her.

Seven held on with only one hand, working the calculator calmly with the other.

Tyla was so well secured in her seat that even the transporter was going to have problems getting her out.

"Ten seconds."

"Eight."

"Seven."

"Six."

Again the ship smashed into a gravitational shift, sending the room sideways.

"Five."

"Hold the thrust," Seven said. "Shut down engines on my command."

"Four."

"Not yet," Seven said to Tyla. "Hold the thrust even."

"Three."

"Perfect," Seven said.

"Two."

"Shut down thrusters."

Tyla's fingers flew over the board, moving like a concert pianist at the top of her form.

"One."

"Thrusters down," Tyla said.

"Let's get out of here," Janeway said.

"Beam out." Chakotay's voice echoed one last time through the thick smell and smoke of the Qavok bridge.

Janeway felt the transporter pull her away.

Then the *Voyager* bridge was under her feet again.

Tyla and Seven stood beside her. All of them were facing the main screen.

"Three seconds," Kim said.

Seven stepped over and glanced at the panel in front of Kim.

"On target and on time, Captain," Seven said.

"Now!" Kim said.

As he spoke, a small white explosion filled the screen near the two neutron stars, then vanished as instantly as it appeared, leaving the swirling forces of the binary behind.

"Seems so small," Tom said.

"Against the power of that binary," Janeway said, "it was nothing more than a small hiccup. But enough of a hiccup to accelerate the mass loss from the bloated secondary and quicken its explosion by exactly two point three nine milliseconds."

"Two point three nine very important milliseconds," Chakotay said.

"When will we know if we've succeeded?" Tyla asked.

"When we can track the path of the neutron star and not one moment before, I'm afraid."

Seven nodded.

"Take us out of here, Tom," Janeway said. "Get us out of this turbulence as quickly as you can."

"Gladly," he said.

Voyager turned and moved away from the binary.

Then, after a moment, Tom said, "Whew, what's that smell?"

He glanced around at Janeway, Seven, and Tyla.

Janeway laughed. It wasn't until Tom had said something that she noticed that all the bridge crew had backed away.

"I think we all need showers and fresh clothes," Janeway said.

"Please," Chakotay said. "Then B'Elanna needs your help, as soon as you can get there. Even without the showers."

"Warp?"

Chakotay nodded.

"Tom, on second thought, once you get us through the turbulence, make the best speed you can away from the binary."

"We won't get far enough, Captain," Seven said. "Using impulse power only."

"I know," Janeway said. "But it will buy us back a few of those milliseconds we just gave away."

CHAPTER 26

B'ELANNA GLANCED UP AS JANEWAY CAME THROUGH the door of Engineering. Her face looked flushed, as if she'd just taken a sonic shower. Maybe she had, for some reason or another.

B'Elanna kept working. So far, so good, on building the new relays for the warp drive. But they could use all the help they could get.

Seven had arrived just a few moments before and gone to work immediately on the repair of the backup relays. She seemed to feel that that was where the best chance of success lay. B'Elanna was still convinced they had to build a new system from scratch.

"What can I do?" Janeway asked. "I know the

three options, three teams. Good thinking on your part."

"Thanks," B'Elanna said.

"My opinion is that the new relay is the best bet," Janeway said. "What can I do?"

"I agree," B'Elanna said. "The group over there needs help finishing those connections while I get this board ready. We're about ten minutes from the first basic test." She glanced up at the wall where she had started a large countdown.

Janeway followed her gaze and nodded.

"Not much time."

"Thirty-six minutes," Janeway said. "More than enough time."

B'Elanna wasn't so sure, but she didn't say anything else aloud. She just nodded and went back to work, pushing even harder than she had been before. But the only problem with working so hard was that time seemed to fly faster.

And right now, that was the last thing she needed.

The bridge was silent as Tyla entered. Dr. Maalot was out of sickbay and at a panel at the back of the room, running figures for something. She couldn't imagine what he might be doing, but she was glad he was up and about.

On the main screen, the binary had gotten smaller as *Voyager* rushed away as fast as its secondary engines would push it. But she knew they could not possibly get ahead of that plasma shock wave from the explosion of the secondary neutron star, let alone the nasty gamma-ray bursts.

"I've gotten shields back up to eighty-three percent," Ensign Kim said.

Commander Chakotay nodded. "Good."

"Ah, Lieutenant Tyla," Dr. Maalot said, turning and smiling. "Good to see you alive."

"And you," she said.

"We are having quite an adventure, aren't we?" he said, smiling as if what they'd been through so far was just a fairy tale.

"I suppose that's one way to look at it," she said. "What are you working on?"

"An idea to help us get out of here alive once more."

"I don't understand," she said.

Commander Chakotay had also overheard the doctor's comments. "You have an idea, Doctor?" Chakotay said, moving up to stand beside Tyla.

"I'm not at all sure it will work."

"Since we're less than twelve minutes away from being destroyed," the commander said, "I'm willing to listen to just about anything."

Tyla was impressed that the commander would, with so little time remaining, be willing to listen to Dr. Maalot. Maalot must have really impressed them earlier.

"Well, as I'm sure you know," Dr. Maalot said, "the leading edge of the coming explosion will be gamma-ray and x-ray photons. Nasty things that will pretty well kill off everybody in this ship if we're not far enough away."

Chakotay nodded.

"Then, following that is a very, very intense plasma shock wave, spreading out at incredible speeds. But not as fast as the first wave, if you get my drift."

Chakotay nodded. "So, if we survive the first blast of gamma-ray photons—"

"And X-rays," Dr. Maalot said.

"—we will have time before the plasma wave. Correct?"

"Exactly. At this distance, we will have an extra ten minutes."

"So how do we survive the first wave?" Tyla asked. She couldn't see a way to do that.

"The best bet would be to get out of the way."

"We're trying to do that, Doctor," Chakotay said, clearly annoyed.

"No, I mean perhaps we could duck in behind something like a large asteroid, a small moon, anything we can find. Let that body take most of the brunt of the shock wave. Then, with *Voyager*'s shields on full, we should make it through. But I need to do a little more figuring."

"Do the math, Doctor," Chakotay said. "Don't let me stop you."

Tyla stepped back against the bulkhead to make sure she also didn't disturb Dr. Maalot.

"Tom, anything like an asteroid or moon nearby?" Chakotay asked, moving down to stand beside his pilot.

"Large asteroid ahead," Tom said. "Seven minutes."

"We've got exactly nine and a half," Chakotay said. "Get us there and in position. Make sure you are ready to jump to warp at any moment. As soon as it comes back on-line."

"Understood, Commander."

Tyla watched as Tom worked, steering the wonderful ship known as *Voyager* as if it was his right hand. She admired his skill.

And envied his position.

Janeway wiped a trickle of sweat from her forehead and glanced up at the clock B'Elanna had on the wall. Five minutes.

Five short minutes.

They didn't have a choice at this moment. They were going to have to try something.

And quickly.

In front of her B'Elanna had her head under the panel. She was hooking up the last connections on their makeshift warp relay.

Seven's group was close to fixing the backup relays. But close wasn't good enough. Close wasn't going to beat the gamma-ray and x-ray bursts that were going to hit the ship in less than five minutes.

"Captain?" Chakotay's voice broke through her thoughts.

"Go ahead."

"We're ducking in behind a large asteroid. Dr. Maalot thinks it might help us ride through the first wave of gamma-rays. That will buy us an extra ten minutes before the plasma wave hits."

"Understood," she said. "Good idea. But stand ready. We're going to try two warp fixes before that point."

"Standing by."

B'Elanna crawled out from under the panel.

"Ready to give it a shot," she said.

"How hard?" Janeway asked. "Warp one for ten seconds won't get us out of the way. Warp six for ten seconds will help a lot."

"Warp six," she said, glancing up at the clock. Janeway followed her gaze. Less than two minutes. This had better work.

Or Dr. Maalot's idea had better work. Right about now they needed one last miracle.

"Janeway to bridge."

"Go ahead, Captain," Chakotay said.

"Warp six. Hit it."

Beside them the panel sparked as the craft jumped to warp six.

"Hold on," B'Elanna said. "Hold on."

A small wisp of smoke drifted up from the panel, but it seemed to be holding.

"Eight seconds," Janeway said.

"Nine."

"Ten."

"Eleven."

"It's holding," B'Elanna said, smiling as the warp drive continued to take them safely away from the impending exploding destruction.

Janeway glanced up at the clock. "Forty-five seconds is all we had left. We cut that very, very close."

"We sure did," B'Elanna said.

On the bridge, Tom glanced around at Chakotay. "Commander, now that we're moving again, exactly where do you want me to go?"

"Away from that neutron star," Chakotay said, smiling and dropping down into his chair. "Just away. We'll circle back to the Lekk home system after we're at a safe distance."

"Sounds wonderful," Tom said.

His hands danced over the control board. "Away it is."

CHAPTER 27

A DAY LATER, LIEUTENANT TYLA STOOD ON THE *Voyager* bridge beside Tuvok, watching as *Voyager* dropped out of warp on the outskirts of her home system. It seemed as if it had been centuries before that that the Qavok had kidnapped her and Dr. Maalot. In her wildest imagination, she never would have thought she would come home in such a fashion. And after having done so much.

The neutron star would soon be a thing of the past. Their tampering had worked. The neutron star wouldn't go near an inhabited system before leaving the galaxy. They had succeeded.

Actually, as Captain Janeway had said, they had gotten very lucky.

Captain Janeway moved up beside her and stood, watching the Lekk system appear on the main screen. She was sipping that foul-smelling liquid they called coffee. It was the only thing on *Voyager* Tyla didn't like, but it was sure making the captain happy.

"Beautiful home you have here," Janeway said between sips as the blue and reddish planet appeared on the screen.

"I've missed it," Tyla said.

"I can imagine," Janeway said.

Tyla noticed that for a moment, Janeway's eyes were distant, as if imagining her own home system so far away.

"Captain," Tyla said. "I don't know how to thank you."

"No need," Janeway said.

"Oh, I must respectfully disagree," Tyla said. "There is a need. You trusted me after I showed you I shouldn't be trusted."

Janeway laughed. "Oh, you could always be trusted," she said, "to do what you needed to do, plus more."

"But my escape attempt?"

"Was what you thought you needed to do," Janeway said, shrugging. "Nothing more and I knew that. The minute you needed to help us, you did, risking your life in the process."

"Well," Tyla said, trying to regain her thoughts after that admission from the captain. "Thank you anyway. From me. And more importantly, from my people."

Janeway nodded. "You're welcome. It feels pretty good, I must admit, to save as many millions of beings as we saved today. Full systems' worth."

"That it does," Tyla said, smiling. At that moment she realized for the first time how good it felt to help others. It was a feeling she would remember.

"Now," Janeway said, "would you like to help us out one more time?"

"Anything."

"It seems my pilot needs a little rest. Would you like to take *Voyager* into your home port?"

Tyla wanted to hug the captain, but instead managed to somehow tone her grin down just enough to say, "I would love to."

"Tom," Janeway said, smiling and patting Tyla on the back, "give her a quick lesson and let her have the helm."

"With pleasure, Captain," he said, standing and stretching as Tyla moved past him and into the *Voyager*'s pilot's chair. She watched him carefully in his instruction, just to make sure there was nothing she missed in his quick directions.

There wasn't. She'd already been watching him long enough to pick it up.

He stepped back. "She's ready. Always was is my guess."

"Are you, Tyla?" Janeway asked.

Tyla felt her heart flutter. Her stomach was clamped tight, but she knew that, without a doubt, she was ready to fly the most majestic and powerful ship she had ever seen.

"Ready."

"Then take us in, Lieutenant Tyla."

"Yes, Captain," Tyla said.

"Voyager to Lekk system control," Tyla said.

"On screen," Janeway said, as she dropped down into her chair behind Tyla and sipped her drink.

"Lekk system control to *Voyager,* you are more than welcome. The entire system is in your debt. Stand by for orbiting instructions."

"Word travels faster than we do, it seems," Chakotay said from beside Janeway.

On the screen Lieutenant Grann's face appeared, all business. Grann and Tyla had gone through the first few years of the service together. He'd ended up in control, she as a pilot.

"Thank you, control," Tyla said, keeping her face very serious. "Standing by."

It took Grann a moment before he looked up. Then it took him another moment to comprehend what he was seeing: a Lekk pilot at the controls of the human ship that had saved their system. And the pilot was Tyla.

His mouth dropped open; then he closed it. Then it dropped open and he let out a little squeak.

Behind Tyla, Janeway, Chakotay, and Ensign Kim laughed.

And Tyla joined them. A natural laugh, the first laugh she'd had in as long as she could remember.

But she knew at that moment, without a doubt, thanks to the humans and their wonderful ship, it would be only the first laugh of many, many to come.

Look for STAR TREK Fiction from Pocket Books

Star Trek®: The Original Series

Star Trek: The Motion Picture • Gene Roddenberry
Star Trek II: The Wrath of Khan • Vonda N. McIntyre
Star Trek III: The Search for Spock • Vonda N. McIntyre
Star Trek IV: The Voyage Home • Vonda N. McIntyre
Star Trek V: The Final Frontier • J. M. Dillard
Star Trek VI: The Undiscovered Country • J. M. Dillard
Star Trek VII: Generations • J. M. Dillard
Enterprise: The First Adventure • Vonda N. McIntyre
Final Frontier • Diane Carey
Strangers from the Sky • Margaret Wander Bonanno
Spock's World • Diane Duane
The Lost Years • J. M. Dillard
Probe • Margaret Wander Bonanno
Prime Directive • Judith and Garfield Reeves-Stevens
Best Destiny • Diane Carey
Shadows on the Sun • Michael Jan Friedman
Sarek • A. C. Crispin
Federation • Judith and Garfield Reeves-Stevens
The Ashes of Eden • William Shatner & Judith and Garfield
    Reeves-Stevens
The Return • William Shatner & Judith and Garfield Reeves-
    Stevens
Star Trek: Starfleet Academy • Diane Carey
Vulcan's Forge • Josepha Sherman and Susan Shwartz
Avenger • William Shatner & Judith and Garfield Reeves-Stevens
Star Trek: Odyssey • William Shatner & Judith and Garfield
    Reeves-Stevens

#1 *Star Trek: The Motion Picture* • Gene Roddenberry
#2 *The Entropy Effect* • Vonda N. McIntyre
#3 *The Klingon Gambit* • Robert E. Vardeman
#4 *The Covenant of the Crown* • Howard Weinstein
#5 *The Prometheus Design* • Sondra Marshak & Myrna
    Culbreath
#6 *The Abode of Life* • Lee Correy
#7 *Star Trek II: The Wrath of Khan* • Vonda N. McIntyre
#8 *Black Fire* • Sonni Cooper

#9 *Triangle* • Sondra Marshak & Myrna Culbreath
#10 *Web of the Romulans* • M. S. Murdock
#11 *Yesterday's Son* • A. C. Crispin
#12 *Mutiny on the Enterprise* • Robert E. Vardeman
#13 *The Wounded Sky* • Diane Duane
#14 *The Trellisane Confrontation* • David Dvorkin
#15 *Corona* • Greg Bear
#16 *The Final Reflection* • John M. Ford
#17 *Star Trek III: The Search for Spock* • Vonda N. McIntyre
#18 *My Enemy, My Ally* • Diane Duane
#19 *The Tears of the Singers* • Melinda Snodgrass
#20 *The Vulcan Academy Murders* • Jean Lorrah
#21 *Uhura's Song* • Janet Kagan
#22 *Shadow Lord* • Laurence Yep
#23 *Ishmael* • Barbara Hambly
#24 *Killing Time* • Della Van Hise
#25 *Dwellers in the Crucible* • Margaret Wander Bonanno
#26 *Pawns and Symbols* • Majiliss Larson
#27 *Mindshadow* • J. M. Dillard
#28 *Crisis on Centaurus* • Brad Ferguson
#29 *Dreadnought!* • Diane Carey
#30 *Demons* • J. M. Dillard
#31 *Battlestations!* • Diane Carey
#32 *Chain of Attack* • Gene DeWeese
#33 *Deep Domain* • Howard Weinstein
#34 *Dreams of the Raven* • Carmen Carter
#35 *The Romulan Way* • Diane Duane & Peter Morwood
#36 *How Much for Just the Planet?* • John M. Ford
#37 *Bloodthirst* • J. M. Dillard
#38 *The IDIC Epidemic* • Jean Lorrah
#39 *Time for Yesterday* • A. C. Crispin
#40 *Timetrap* • David Dvorkin
#41 *The Three-Minute Universe* • Barbara Paul
#42 *Memory Prime* • Judith and Garfield Reeves-Stevens
#43 *The Final Nexus* • Gene DeWeese
#44 *Vulcan's Glory* • D. C. Fontana
#45 *Double, Double* • Michael Jan Friedman
#46 *The Cry of the Onlies* • Judy Klass
#47 *The Kobayashi Maru* • Julia Ecklar
#48 *Rules of Engagement* • Peter Morwood
#49 *The Pandora Principle* • Carolyn Clowes
#50 *Doctor's Orders* • Diane Duane
#51 *Enemy Unseen* • V. E. Mitchell

#52 *Home Is the Hunter* • Dana Kramer Rolls
#53 *Ghost-Walker* • Barbara Hambly
#54 *A Flag Full of Stars* • Brad Ferguson
#55 *Renegade* • Gene DeWeese
#56 *Legacy* • Michael Jan Friedman
#57 *The Rift* • Peter David
#58 *Face of Fire* • Michael Jan Friedman
#59 *The Disinherited* • Peter David
#60 *Ice Trap* • L. A. Graf
#61 *Sanctuary* • John Vornholt
#62 *Death Count* • L. A. Graf
#63 *Shell Game* • Melissa Crandall
#64 *The Starship Trap* • Mel Gilden
#65 *Windows on a Lost World* • V. E. Mitchell
#66 *From the Depths* • Victor Milan
#67 *The Great Starship Race* • Diane Carey
#68 *Firestorm* • L. A. Graf
#69 *The Patrian Transgression* • Simon Hawke
#70 *Traitor Winds* • L. A. Graf
#71 *Crossroad* • Barbara Hambly
#72 *The Better Man* • Howard Weinstein
#73 *Recovery* • J. M. Dillard
#74 *The Fearful Summons* • Denny Martin Flynn
#75 *First Frontier* • Diane Carey & Dr. James I. Kirkland
#76 *The Captain's Daughter* • Peter David
#77 *Twilight's End* • Jerry Oltion
#78 *The Rings of Tautee* • Dean W. Smith & Kristine K. Rusch
#79 *Invasion #1: First Strike* • Diane Carey
#80 *The Joy Machine* • James Gunn
#81 *Mudd in Your Eye* • Jerry Oltion
#82 *Mind Meld* • John Vornholt
#83 *Heart of the Sun* • Pamela Sargent & George Zebrowski
#84 *Assignment: Eternity* • Greg Cox

Star Trek: The Next Generation®

Encounter at Farpoint • David Gerrold
Unification • Jeri Taylor
Relics • Michael Jan Friedman
Descent • Diane Carey
All Good Things • Michael Jan Friedman
Star Trek: Klingon • Dean W. Smith & Kristine K. Rusch
Star Trek VII: Generations • J. M. Dillard
Metamorphosis • Jean Lorrah
Vendetta • Peter David
Reunion • Michael Jan Friedman
Imzadi • Peter David
The Devil's Heart • Carmen Carter
Dark Mirror • Diane Duane
Q-Squared • Peter David
Crossover • Michael Jan Friedman
Kahless • Michael Jan Friedman
Star Trek: First Contact • J. M. Dillard
The Best and the Brightest • Susan Wright
Planet X • Michael Jan Friedman

#1 *Ghost Ship* • Diane Carey
#2 *The Peacekeepers* • Gene DeWeese
#3 *The Children of Hamlin* • Carmen Carter
#4 *Survivors* • Jean Lorrah
#5 *Strike Zone* • Peter David
#6 *Power Hungry* • Howard Weinstein
#7 *Masks* • John Vornholt
#8 *The Captains' Honor* • David and Daniel Dvorkin
#9 *A Call to Darkness* • Michael Jan Friedman
#10 *A Rock and a Hard Place* • Peter David
#11 *Gulliver's Fugitives* • Keith Sharee
#12 *Doomsday World* • David, Carter, Friedman & Greenberg
#13 *The Eyes of the Beholders* • A. C. Crispin
#14 *Exiles* • Howard Weinstein
#15 *Fortune's Light* • Michael Jan Friedman
#16 *Contamination* • John Vornholt
#17 *Boogeymen* • Mel Gilden
#18 *Q-in-Law* • Peter David

#19 *Perchance to Dream* • Howard Weinstein
#20 *Spartacus* • T. L. Mancour
#21 *Chains of Command* • W. A. McCay & E. L. Flood
#22 *Imbalance* • V. E. Mitchell
#23 *War Drums* • John Vornholt
#24 *Nightshade* • Laurell K. Hamilton
#25 *Grounded* • David Bischoff
#26 *The Romulan Prize* • Simon Hawke
#27 *Guises of the Mind* • Rebecca Neason
#28 *Here There Be Dragons* • John Peel
#29 *Sins of Commission* • Susan Wright
#30 *Debtors' Planet* • W. R. Thompson
#31 *Foreign Foes* • David Galanter & Greg Brodeur
#32 *Requiem* • Michael Jan Friedman & Kevin Ryan
#33 *Balance of Power* • Dafydd ab Hugh
#34 *Blaze of Glory* • Simon Hawke
#35 *The Romulan Stratagem* • Robert Greenberger
#36 *Into the Nebula* • Gene DeWeese
#37 *The Last Stand* • Brad Ferguson
#38 *Dragon's Honor* • Kij Johnson & Greg Cox
#39 *Rogue Saucer* • John Vornholt
#40 *Possession* • J. M. Dillard & Kathleen O'Malley
#41 *Invasion #2: The Soldiers of Fear* • Dean W. Smith & Kristine K. Rusch
#42 *Infiltrator* • W. R. Thompson
#43 *A Fury Scorned* • Pam Sargent & George Zebrowski
#44 *The Death of Princes* • John Peel
#45 *Intellivore* • Diane Duane
#46 *To Storm Heaven* • Esther Friesner
#47 *Q Continuum #1: Q-Space* • Greg Cox
#48 *Q Continuum #2: Q-Zone* • Greg Cox
#49 *Q Continuum #3: Q-Strike* • Greg Cox

Star Trek: Deep Space Nine®

The Search • Diane Carey
Warped • K. W. Jeter
The Way of the Warrior • Diane Carey
Star Trek: Klingon • Dean W. Smith & Kristine K. Rusch
Trials and Tribble-ations • Diane Carey
Far Beyond the Stars • Steve Barnes

#1 *Emissary* • J. M. Dillard
#2 *The Siege* • Peter David
#3 *Bloodletter* • K. W. Jeter
#4 *The Big Game* • Sandy Schofield
#5 *Fallen Heroes* • Dafydd ab Hugh
#6 *Betrayal* • Lois Tilton
#7 *Warchild* • Esther Friesner
#8 *Antimatter* • John Vornholt
#9 *Proud Helios* • Melissa Scott
#10 *Valhalla* • Nathan Archer
#11 *Devil in the Sky* • Greg Cox & John Greggory Betancourt
#12 *The Laertian Gamble* • Robert Sheckley
#13 *Station Rage* • Diane Carey
#14 *The Long Night* • Dean W. Smith & Kristine K. Rusch
#15 *Objective: Bajor* • John Peel
#16 *Invasion #3: Time's Enemy* • L. A. Graf
#17 *The Heart of the Warrior* • John Greggory Betancourt
#18 *Saratoga* • Michael Jan Friedman
#19 *The Tempest* • Susan Wright
#20 *Wrath of the Prophets* • P. David, M. J. Friedman,
    R. Greenberger
#21 *Trial by Error* • Mark Garland
#22 *Vengeance* • Dafydd ab Hugh
#23 *Rebels Book 1* • Dafydd ab Hugh
#24 *Rebels Book 2* • Dafydd ab Hugh
#25 *Rebels Book 3* • Dafydd ab Hugh

Star Trek®: Voyager™

Flashback • Diane Carey
Mosaic • Jeri Taylor
The Black Shore • Greg Cox

#1 *Caretaker* • L. A. Graf
#2 *The Escape* • Dean W. Smith & Kristine K. Rusch
#3 *Ragnarok* • Nathan Archer
#4 *Violations* • Susan Wright
#5 *Incident at Arbuk* • John Greggory Betancourt
#6 *The Murdered Sun* • Christie Golden
#7 *Ghost of a Chance* • Mark A. Garland & Charles G. McGraw
#8 *Cybersong* • S. N. Lewitt
#9 *Invasion #4: The Final Fury* • Dafydd ab Hugh
#10 *Bless the Beasts* • Karen Haber
#11 *The Garden* • Melissa Scott
#12 *Chrysalis* • David Niall Wilson
#13 *The Black Shore* • Greg Cox
#14 *Marooned* • Christie Golden
#15 *Echoes* • Dean W. Smith & Kristine K. Rusch
#16 *Seven of Nine* • Christie Golden
#17 *Death of a Neutron Star* • Eric Kotani

Star Trek®: New Frontier

#1 *House of Cards* • Peter David
#2 *Into the Void* • Peter David
#3 *The Two-Front War* • Peter David
#4 *End Game* • Peter David
#5 *Martyr* • Peter David
#6 *Fire on High* • Peter David

Star Trek®: Day of Honor

Book One: *Ancient Blood* • Diane Carey
Book Two: *Armageddon Sky* • L. A. Graf
Book Three: *Her Klingon Soul* • Michael Jan Friedman
Book Four: *Treaty's Law* • Dean W. Smith & Kristine K. Rusch

Star Trek®: The Captain's Table

Book One: *War Dragons* • L. A. Graf
Book Two: *Dujonian's Hoard* • Michael Jan Friedman
Book Three: *The Mist* • Dean W. Smith & Kristine K. Rusch
Book Four: *Fire Ship* • Diane Carey
Book Five: *Once Burned* • Peter David
Book Six: *Where Sea Meets Sky* • Jerry Oltion

Star Trek®: The Dominion War

Book One: *Behind Enemy Lines* • John Vornholt
Book Two: *Call to Arms* • Diane Carey
Book Three: *A Tunnel Through the Stars* • John Vornholt
Book Four: *Sacrifice of Angels* • John Carey

Star Trek®: My Brother's Keeper

Book One: *Republic* • Michael Jan Friedman
Book Two: *Constitution* • Michael Jan Friedman
Book Three: *Enterprise* • Michael Jan Friedman

Shattered Light™
A Mystical Quest

The world of Delos could soon be yours. This spring, Simon & Schuster Interactive, Pocket Books, and Five to Midnight will bring you *Shattered Light*. Immerse yourself in this fantastical world through novels and a CD-ROM game for the PC from Catware. Use the game's exclusive "world builder" software to create your own fantasy experience and then join your friends online. Look for *Shattered Light* in March.

Online.

At bookstores.

At software stores.

Everywhere!

Look for the online version at
America's newest gamesite:
Five to Midnight.
www.Shatteredlight.com